CULLEN

EVIE MONROE

Copyright and Disclaimer

This book is a work of fiction. The names, characters, places and incidents are products of the writer's imagination and have been used fictitiously and are not to be construed as real. Any resemblance to persons, living or dead, actual events, locales or organizations is entirely coincidental.

Copyright © 2018 Book Boyfriends Publishing

All rights reserved. No part of this publication may be reproduced, stored in or introduced into a retrieval system, or transmitted, in any form, or by any means (electronic, mechanical, photocopying, recording, or otherwise) without the prior written permission of the copyright owner. The author acknowledges the trademarked status and trademark owners of various products referenced in this work of fiction, which have been used without permission. The publication/use of the trademarks is not authorized, associated with, or sponsored by the trademark owners.

Table of Contents

Copyright and Disclaimer ii

Chapter One 7

Chapter Two 19

Chapter Three 35

Chapter Four 53

Chapter Five 75

Chapter Six 89

Chapter Seven 103

Chapter Eight 109

Chapter Nine 117

Chapter Ten 129

Chapter Eleven 143

Chapter Twelve 153

Chapter Thirteen 171

Chapter Fourteen 181

Chapter Fifteen 187

Chapter Sixteen 203

Chapter Seventeen 213

Chapter Eighteen 227

Chapter Nineteen 235

Chapter Twenty 245

Chapter Twenty-One 253

Chapter Twenty-Two 277

Chapter Twenty-Three 299

Chapter Twenty-Four 309

Chapter Twenty-Five 313

Chapter Twenty-Six 321

Chapter Twenty-Seven 329

Chapter Twenty-Eight 339

Chapter Twenty-Nine 365

Chapter Thirty 381

Cullen

Steel Cobras MC Book 2

By Evie Monroe

Cover Model: Josh Mario John

Photographer: Lane Dorsey

CULLEN

Chapter One

Cullen

Just what I liked. Sitting around a table across from the rest of the club, with our thumbs up our asses.

That wasn't how I usually operated my Steel Cobras. We were fierce. Made big plays with high risks. Kicked ass and took names.

But we sat there now, giving each other stupid looks, because no one wanted to admit it. We didn't know what our rival motorcycle club, Hell's Fury, was up to.

They'd been quiet for the past few weeks, ever since we offed Blaze, their leader, and tore them new assholes. They'd run for the hills, crying for their mamas.

But their silence was suspicious.

"I tell you, they're planning something," Phoenix, the VP of our club, and my best friend, said. "We need to act. Crush them. This won't be over 'til they're all dead."

Easy for him to say. He'd wanted to destroy our rival club ever since they'd snapped up his girl, Olivia, to use for bait. They nearly killed her. For the last two weeks, he'd been preaching No Mercy when it came to Hell's Fury.

His bloodthirst was beginning to spread. Now Jet, Phoenix's little brother, and Drake, both officers in the Cobras, were starting to echo those sentiments.

Which meant I, as President of the Cobras, needed to shut this shit down before it got worse.

I held out my hands as the men raged around one another, jumping off their seats, at each other's throats. I didn't raise my voice. I found that I didn't need to. "Men. Sit the fuck down."

Phoenix—also known as Nix—was as loyal a motherfucker as there could be, always listening, respecting the club. Once he sat his ass down, the rest of the men fell in like dominos.

I pulled up off of the chair I was backwards-straddling and took a drag of my cigarette. I moved to the front of the room in the warehouse we'd recently moved into as our clubhouse. For the past two years, since I'd become president, we'd been having the meetings at my house. That all ended about a month ago, when Hell's Fury decided to pay us a little unfriendly visit.

A month later, and I was still pulling bullets out of my fucking hot tub.

The warehouse was good. Quiet. On the end of the pier in Aveline Bay. We could park our bikes out there, make all the noise we wanted, and not have to worry about the Fury sneaking up on us.

"Guys," I said, pacing in front of them. "Just because they're quiet doesn't mean they're not planning something. And we can't just go in there, guns blazing. They showed us they had the numbers. Even if they've lost half their guys, they're still bigger than us."

Drake shook his head. "They're planning something. But we need to strike while their numbers are down and put an end to them for good."

Hart looked up from his computer. "I haven't seen any chatter at all online. Not a single one. But I don't want to dare think they're done."

"Hell, no, they're not done," Zain said. "They're biding their time. You can bet on that."

I looked at Zain, who was holding his side, having just recovered from a serious gunshot wound. Zain was one of the newer members of the club, but a man I could trust. He had the most intelligence on Hell's Fury, because he'd almost been a part of them. That was, until Blaze fucked him over by stealing his girl. After that, he came to me. Though I'd kept his dealings with the Fury secret from the other Cobras, I trusted his point of view on them.

"Right. But it doesn't mean we got to go out and fight without knowing what we're up against."

CULLEN

"Yeah, it does," Nix said, not looking up from the text he was thumbing in. I'd bet a thousand bucks he was texting his girl Olivia. "We get 'em now, while they're weak. We made the mistake last time of not stamping them out, and they grew. We need to take them out."

"I'm not running out there blind," I said. "We need to know what we're dealing with. Come on, assholes. Let's vote."

They all gathered in the circle.

I said, "All in favor of retaliation right now. Show of hands."

Nix, Jet and Drake all raised their hands.

"All for waiting it out until we got some real info?"

Hart and Zain lifted their hands. I raised mine to join them.

"Three v. three. But the final call goes to me." As president, the final call always went to me. But I needed to know where they stood.

I looked them over. Jet had a face that could do no wrong. Hart was our tech guy. The babies of the club. "You two," I said. "I want you to go out and snoop around. Go to their clubhouse, and the places they usually hang out. Ask questions. See what you can find."

They both nodded.

"I'll call church again later this week, and we'll make a final decision then," I said, standing up. "All right. That's it. If no one has anything else, I'll talk to you all later."

They stood up and started to disperse. I called Nix over as he was pulling his leather jacket over his thick arms. "How's your girl?"

He lifted his chin, baring the tat at his throat. "Liv? She's good. But you know her. She's out for blood when it comes to the Fury."

I smirked. "That's why we like her." I flicked the ashes of my cigarette away. "You moving in with her now?"

CULLEN

He nodded.

"Man. You've gone soft. Never thought I'd see you fucking whipped." I shook my head. "Who am I gonna go out Friday nights with?"

He crossed his arms. "Hunting pussy? Last I saw, you didn't have to hunt. I thought all the gingers in the world just lined up for you."

"Nah. Not just that." I waved him off. Still, I was bummed I wouldn't have him on Friday nights. Of all the guys, he was the one I could chill with.

But those days were coming to an end. I knew they would—Nix may have talked a good game, but he'd wanted a woman, and found her.

Easy pussy—that was what I wanted, and that was what I'd always want, 'til the day I died. I might've been thirty now, but I showed no signs of change on that front. I had too much else on my mind with the Cobras to deal with any of that.

Which reminded me. I really could've used some easy pussy right now. My muscles were tight with tension. It wasn't one of the best times for the Cobras. We'd almost lost a few men after the skirmish with the Fury, and I wasn't so stupid to think this was the end. Something was brewing, and I needed my club to be safe.

Phoebe. I'd call Phoebe.

I told Nix I'd see him later, then got on my bike and took off down the pier, toward home. I drove past The Wall, our local watering hole, but was too tired to even stop in and hang with the other Cobras I knew would be there. I went straight home, still thinking of the Fury.

We would eventually rumble again. It was only a matter of time.

I rode up to my house overlooking the Pacific and the garage door opened automatically to let me in. The guys had joked once that this was my own Bat Cave, and I liked that. That was, until the Fury ripped it apart a few weeks ago. I pulled off my helmet and walked into the living room of the darkened house. The carpet was ripped up everywhere, and the furniture covered in

CULLEN

tarp and piled in the center of the room to allow for painting. So I navigated around the mess, turning on lights as I went.

I strode into the kitchen, opened the fridge, and pulled out a Coors. Taking a swig, I put my phone on speaker on the center island and dialed up my interior designer.

She answered on the first ring. "Cullen?"

"Yeah baby," I said. "What're you doing?"

"Nothing much," she said. "I'm—"

"Then you're doing it with me. Get your ass over here."

I ended the call and frowned at the stack of mail brought in from the housekeeper. Decided to ignore it. Phoebe would be over in ten, probably, in some little get-up that she'd bought at the lingerie store with lots of ribbons and lace. As if I cared about any of that. She was a hell of an interior designer, a hell of a good fuck who was up for anything, and she had red hair.

She'd be good for what ailed me.

Other than that, I didn't give a shit.

Yawning, I climbed the stairs up to my bedroom, ripping off my t-shirt so I could change into a different one.

As I did, the doorbell rang.

I looked at my phone. Three minutes. Phoebe was just a few doors down, shacking up with her doctor husband, but that was a new world record, even for her.

I reached for the door handle and pulled it open. "Hey, baby, you excited or—"

I stopped. It wasn't Phoebe, with her pale skin, hair all done up, dressed in her hot little outfit.

The only thing the same was that this girl's hair was red.

She was probably the only redhead whose name I'd never forget.

Grace Wilson.

And she was holding a kid.

CULLEN

My eyes went from her big blue ones, to the baby, and then back to hers again. I couldn't find the air to breathe.

"Oh fuck," I said.

EVIE MONROE

CULLEN

Chapter Two

Grace

When I pulled up at the house that belonged to my ex, my stomach dropped.

He was such an absolute dickwad.

A spoiled, rich, hot-as-fuck dickwad.

And the house? Gorgeous. Overlooking the Pacific cliffs, with a wall and turrets, lush landscaping and sprawling wings. Cullen McKnight, rough, dirty, no-good biker with a penchant for cheap women and loud parties lived *here*?

I checked the address I'd gotten from a friend of a friend and asked the cabbie, "You sure this is 1212 Riviera Way?"

He nodded.

Hmm. Maybe the friend of a friend had been playing jokes on me. "There isn't some other 1212 Riviera Way, is—"

"No," the man said to me in a heavy Spanish accent. "This is it."

I took a deep breath, remembering the last time I saw Cullen. His living arrangement a little over two years ago had been a dirty basement apartment where his master bed was also the living room sofa.

Then I remembered reading something about him in the newspaper. He'd never said as much to me, but his father was Brent McKnight. Yes, *the* Brent McKnight, lead guitarist for the 80's hair band The Fritz. He died in a drug overdose about two months after I'd left and his only heir? Just happened to be Cullen.

Or so the story went.

I couldn't be sure. All he'd ever said was that he and his dad weren't on speaking terms. And one thing the dickwad wasn't, was verbose.

But this? It could've been a millionaire rock star's house. It looked flashy enough.

CULLEN

The cab driver cleared his throat. "You gonna get out, or you just gonna sit there staring at it all day?"

I gnawed on my lip as I checked the meter. $18.30. Stay or go, that was the question. It'd have been a tough decision, if I didn't have only twenty dollars to my name.

I forked over the crumpled bill, studying the house, really hoping the jerk was home. It was a long walk back to the homeless shelter downtown, and my feet already hurt from pounding the pavement, looking for work.

As I grabbed the handle and pushed open the car door, a light in the foyer went on. I could see the shape of someone moving through the sidelights by the door.

That was a good sign.

He was home. Maybe not alone, but still home.

I didn't care if he had a dozen girls living with him, which frankly, I wouldn't put past him. I just needed one of those bedrooms. Maybe a little cash. That was all.

EVIE MONROE

The cabbie gave me my change and I hoisted my bag onto my back. Then I reached beside me and bundled Ella into my arms. She looked up at me through the shadows like, *Shouldn't I be asleep already, momma?*

I kissed her forehead, savoring her sweet smell. *Yes, soon. We're gonna find you a safe place to rest.*

I didn't just want that. I wanted her to have safety, permanence, love—all the things I never had growing up. But right now, I'd settle for sleep.

"Thanks," I said to the cabbie, bumping the door closed with my hip.

I wavered on my feet with the weight of the heavy backpack containing everything I owned, and the eighteen-month-old baby in my arms. She was all I cared about in this world. I walked up the winding path to the front door and pressed the doorbell with my elbow.

Cullen never did anything fast. He always had this easy, fuck-it-all way about him. So I was surprised

CULLEN

when he ripped open the door, right away, a surly smile on his face. He said, "Hey, baby, you—"

And then he stopped. His smile faded.

Didn't take a genius to know he'd been expecting someone else. Someone female, probably red-haired, built like a thoroughbred, with curves to kill for.

Same old Cullen.

Those killer silver-blue eyes went from me, to Ella.

"Holy fuck," he breathed out.

I wished he looked like a piece of shit. But no, these past two years had clearly been good to him. He was tattooed, built and sexy, with a full beard and a brooding stare. He'd let his hair grow out a bit, a lock of his dirty blond curls sweeping down the center of his forehead.

"Holy? You flatter me. The fuck wasn't all *that* good," I said, adjusting Ella in my arms as she tugged on my no-frills ponytail. "Hello, Cullen."

He turned away from me, showing off his strong, muscular back. Just what I didn't need to see. His gorgeous, ripped abs and hard chest, covered in tattoos, which was what got me in this trouble in the first place.

Me? I was a hell of a lot softer, and, well, chubbier than he'd last seen me. Despite going to bed hungry a lot more, I still hadn't been able to lose the baby weight.

It just made me hate myself more as I stood in front of him, opening myself up to his inspection.

I opened my mouth to speak, but he beat me to it. He scrubbed both hands through his dirty blonde hair and turned back to me. "What are you doing here?" His eyes fell on Ella. "And what the hell is that?"

"*That*?" I was hit for the first time since I left him with a feeling I'd almost forgotten. The inexplicable rage only he could light in me. "Damn, Cullen, you are such a charmer."

His upper lip curled in a snarl.

CULLEN

"She's not a *that*. She's a *she*. Her name is Ella. And I'm not sure. But I think she might be a baby."

"Funny. Yours?"

"Actually, she's the latest fashion accessory. Everyone's carrying one around these days."

Typical, he never reacted to any of my quips. He looked her over, from her chubby little toes to her pretty bow lips, to her bright blue eyes. No one could say that Ella wasn't gorgeous. Complete strangers stopped me in the street to tell me how beautiful she was. She had a magnetism people just wanted to be around.

Well, except for the dickwad in front of me.

He took a step back.

"*Why* are you here, Grace?"

I was pleased he remembered my name. That was a feat for Cullen. There was no doubt in my mind he'd probably had a hundred girls in the two plus years since I stormed out of his apartment, each one with bigger tits than the next. I bet he'd never even found out their names before fucking them. He probably didn't even make it into bed with most of them; he probably just fucked them in an alley somewhere.

I knew this, because I knew Cullen. We had a relationship that lasted six whole months, and that was the longest he'd ever been with the same woman.

He was more than a player. He was the champion of the game.

It was starting to get cold outside, and the wind off the ocean was whipping up something fierce. Everything I was carrying was slowly and surely weighing me down, so much so I was about three seconds away from falling into an ugly heap on the floor. I pointed into his white foyer, complete with fancy crystal chandelier, which seemed so, I didn't know. *Anti*-Cullen? "Can I come in?"

He ran his tongue over his top teeth and gazed out the door, past me. Then he scratched at the back of his head and flattened himself against the door to let me pass. "Yeah. For a minute."

CULLEN

I walked inside, gnawing on my cheek as I moved much too close to his chest. I didn't want to do it. I hated being at Cullen McKnight's mercy for anything. I'd been there before, and it was like extricating myself from a massive spider web. But I had no choice, now. Nowhere to go. No one to turn to.

I looked around—the foyer was sparkly. Through an arched doorway, I spotted a granite kitchen countertop, covered fully in all the kinds of bottles I'd expect from Cullen—Tito's Vodka, Patron, Fireball, Jack, as well as an assortment of empty beer bottles. He didn't talk much about his past, but he had told me he'd grown up with his father having parties all the time. I bet this was just normal for him. "I heard about your dad. I'm sorry."

He shrugged. "I'm not."

"I thought you'd go and sell this place. It's not really you, is it?"

He studied me. "How do you know what I am?"

EVIE MONROE

I frowned. Correction: I'd *known* Cullen. Maybe I didn't know him anymore. "I guess I don't."

He let in a breath, as Ella stopped looking in wonder at the chandelier and started to whine. He pointed to the door. "All right, well, nice catching up, but—"

"How about if I stay a little longer than a minute?" I blurted.

He closed the door and turned to me, eyebrow raised.

My eyes trailed to the floor. And then it all just poured out: "I had a place to live. A reliable sitter. A car. But then I lost my job. I couldn't afford rent. I sold my car and have been staying in a hotel, until I couldn't afford that. I stayed one night at the shelter, but I don't want to go back. It's not safe there for Ella. I wouldn't ask you unless I really needed it, Cullen. Please."

I swallowed the bile in my throat. I hated begging Cullen for anything.

CULLEN

His eyes narrowed. "You're telling me you got nowhere to go?"

I nodded. Ella blew a raspberry with her cute little lips and gave him one of her killer smiles.

Oblivious, he stalked past us, into his kitchen. I followed behind him. Jesus, every surface was covered in bottles. I plopped Ella down on his clean white floor and let the backpack drop to the ground with a thud. Then I lifted Ella back into my arms. When I joined him in the kitchen, he was chugging a beer.

"So, is that a yes?"

He just stared at me, mouth full of beer, lips still wrapped around the bottleneck.

He finally swallowed. "I don't know, girl. I'm in the middle of things."

I looked around. He sure was. The kitchen showed he was in the middle of drinking himself to death. The living room had been gutted, and everything was covered in tarps. It looked like he was doing some serious renovations. "I don't care. You can put me and

Ella in one of the rooms upstairs and I swear, we won't make a noise. Or if not, call me a cab and give me cash for a hotel room and—"

Suddenly, the doorbell rang.

Cullen tossed his beer bottle in the sink with a loud crash that made Ella jump and she let out a yell. He didn't notice. He strutted in his fine jeans, slung low on his perfect ass, back to the front door. I tried not to salivate over that tight waist and little curved area with the two dimples, right above the swell of his ass as he pulled the door open.

I was expecting either a girly little giggle, or a sexy purr. Cullen didn't discriminate. I got both. A giggle-purr. I watched as his flavor of the week—or maybe just the night?— strutted in, throwing her arms around him. He murmured something to her, and she said, "Oh? Then why did you . . ."

"Come on," he barked.

I heard her heels clicking on the floor as she came closer. When she appeared, clinging tight to Cullen's

CULLEN

side, she wasn't too far off from what I was picturing. Too much red hair. Big boobs, pushed up to her chin. Legs for miles. Practically no clothes.

She took one look at me and frowned. "Cullen. I don't do the threesome thing."

"Whoa," I said, looking at Cullen. "Neither do I."

"That makes three of us," Cullen said under his breath. Ugh, I couldn't believe I'd wasted an egg on this guy. He cleared his throat. "Phoebe, this is Grace. Grace, this is Phoebe, my interior designer."

Right. His interior designer. I tried to suppress a snort, but it came out anyway. "You've done wonders with the place."

Cullen scowled at me and took my elbow. "Grace was just leaving."

Bastard. I frowned and picked up Ella, who slumped her head against my chest. I hated making this such a long night for her. All she wanted to do was go to sleep.

And the dickwad was kicking us out so he could get his fuck on.

He motioned me forward and reached into the pocket of his jeans for his wallet. He grabbed my bag and pulled out two hundred dollars as he walked me toward the door.

Dropping the bag at the door, he handed me the money and reached for his phone, dialing up a number. As it rang, he lifted his chin from the receiver and said, "Once you get through with this money, are you gonna be right back in the same spot?"

I didn't want to say yes, but, yes. There was no doubt. It was impossible to find a job with a kid and no money. I nodded.

By then he was already on the phone with the cab company. He gave them the address and hung up. Then he reached into his wallet and pulled out another two hundred, as Phoebe called to him from the living room.

"Cullen! You called me over here. Don't make me wait."

CULLEN

His gorgeous blue eyes were distracted from me for a split second. Then he said, "Where's your grandmother?"

"She died," I mumbled. "Over a year ago."

I didn't expect a sympathy card from Cullen for the death of my last remaining relative, and I didn't get one. He gazed in concentration at Ella. "What about its father? What the hell's he doing about this?"

I looked up at him, then back at Ella, trying to keep the tears from my eyes. I did not need to cry now. But Cullen could be so dense, sometimes. Didn't he see that his daughter had his exact same, piercing silver-blue eyes? She even had that little dimple, right on the center of her chin. I used to stare at it with adoration when we spent long, lazy mornings in bed together.

In the silence, it suddenly dawned on him. Cullen wasn't easy to surprise. He never showed a ripple. All I got was a slight widening of the eyes.

He leaned his thick arm against the wall above him and raked a hand through the wild blonde hair. His voice was low, barely a breath. "You're fucking kidding me, right?"

I shook my head.

"She's yours, Cullen," I said finally. "Ella is yours."

Chapter Three

Cullen

My dick shriveled in my pants as my eyes swept over the kid.

The kid who Grace Wilson said was mine.

The kid who couldn't be mine.

My life started to flash in front of my eyes, but I held that back. I refused to give in. Refused to accept my life was over.

We'd used protection, every time. I was sure of it. I was a fucking boy scout in the protection department, because the only thing I didn't want more than a steady woman was a baby.

Fucking hell.

Suddenly, I was back at my little sister Aria's place downtown. I'd rented that piece of shit apartment while I was getting my shit together, since I'd had it with my dad's nightly drug parties. The man was sixty, and still having orgies in the fucking living room like some fucking twenty-year old hippie. He'd fucking disgusted me, but the final straw was when I came home to find my place in the pool house ransacked and a lot of my shit, and the thousands of dollars of cash I'd accumulated, taken. My father didn't even care.

Aria's little shithole *was,* in every sense of the word, a shithole, but it was freedom. Working at the Lucky Leaf Garage fixing motorcycles, I didn't have a lot of extra cash yet. I'd been with the Cobras a while by then, and had a good chance at being named president, and hadn't wanted to be still living at home, anyway.

I met Grace three days after I moved in. She was Aria's next-door neighbor and friend. I caught her looking at me from the outside steps of her house when I was moving boxes in, wearing these short-shorts and little halter top that had her taut stomach on display and full tits, with her nipples poking out. Strawberry blonde hair that fell in two pigtails, nearly down to her waist. She was a little spitfire of a girl, barely five feet tall, and all mouth. She lived with her grandmother and sometimes, I'd lean against the wall and listen to her screaming her head off at the poor old lady.

One night, she'd come over for a talk with Aria, but Aria was at work. The way she licked her lips, though, I knew she'd come for me. I let her in and we had a few beers.

Then, somehow, I lured her down to my basement, and she didn't leave for the next three days.

We just fucked. Again and again and again, our bodies so in tune with each other, we couldn't get enough. It was like a daze, a whirlwind. I'd never felt anything like that, before or since.

So, now, thinking back on it, one of those times might not have been protected.

Shit.

I bit down hard, trying not to think of those three days, and the six months afterward. The six months in my entire life that had been different. That had felt … I wasn't sure how to describe it. Just different. In a way I never wanted to feel ever again.

Fuck that. Not with anyone, but especially not with her. She fucking left me. No woman left me and got a second chance.

"You left me in the middle of the night," I bit out, drawing a hand over my face. "You didn't fucking return my calls."

She nodded. "I know. I'm sorry."

"Sorry? What the—?" I fisted my hands as Phoebe appeared in the doorway. She'd undone the tie to her coat and was wearing something red, that bared too much of her fine parts.

But my dick was completely dead.

I had a kid. My dick was hanging its head in shame.

Phoebe started to give me a come-hither look but I met that with a scowl that effectively shot that down. I held up a finger to her. "Don't." I growled. "Just. Go home."

Phoebe let out a sigh and put her hands on her hips. "Wait, are you telling me—"

CULLEN

I pointed at her. Then the door. "Yes. Go."

I reached for it, swung it open, and stepped aside. As I did, a cab pulled into the driveway, its headlights sweeping across Grace's face. She took a step toward it.

I pointed at Grace. "You. Stay."

Grace shook her head. "Do you really think ordering women around like they're dogs is going to work for you?"

I scowled at her as Phoebe, without another word, scurried out the door, between us. She kissed her finger, pressed it to my bottom lip and said, "Call me again, baby."

I raised an eyebrow at Grace. "Always has."

"Well, not with me it doesn't," she said, thrusting her chin out and reaching for the door. Leave it to Grace Fucking Wilson to act like a princess even when she had absolutely nothing. I held her elbow.

"Tell me why you left, first."

She sighed, hedged. Looked down at her kid—our kid—and gnawed on her lip some more. "I had a good reason to. Really."

"Yeah? Well, I'd like to hear it. And I'd also like to hear why you thought it wasn't necessary to tell me I'm a dad until now?"

Just then, the little girl lifted her head off Grace's shoulder and yawned sleepily. Grace stroked her head. "Do you think I could lay her down somewhere first?"

I shrugged. She'd put me off for almost two years. Another few minutes wouldn't hurt. I led her upstairs and into one of the guest rooms. Which happened to be the room on the other end of the house, furthest from mine. I flipped on the light and she looked around.

She dropped her backpack on the bed.

"I'll be back in a minute," I muttered, cursing to myself as I went outside to send the cab away.

As I did, I thought of that last night we were together. We'd been lying in my lumpy old futon at the shithole, and she was on top of me, naked, and I was inside her. She was doing that mesmerizing little dance she did, rubbing her perfect little body on mine, making herself feel good, her tits swaying in time to her movements.

Then my cell phone rang, and I saw in the darkness that it was Nix.

I'd been waiting all day for his call. Waiting for word on a car we were loading overseas.

And I made my first mistake.

I went to answer it. As I lifted it, she grabbed it from my hand and held it over my head, taunting me.

I motioned to her, serious. "Give me that."

She grinned. "Nope. Make me come first. I'm close."

I dug my fingers into her thighs to get her to stop. "GIVE. THAT. TO. ME."

She stopped moving on top of me and tossed it across the room, a triumphant look on her face.

"What the . . .?" I lifted her off of my dick and scrambled across the room to pick it up. I answered it just in time and made the plans to meet Nix at the dock in a half hour. Then I turned to her. "What the fuck is wrong with you?"

The girl had blue eyes that could turn to fire. Nothing any woman could do hit me quite like Grace's eyes. She snapped, "What the fuck is wrong with me? What the fuck is wrong with you? I thought we were— I don't know—in the middle of something important?" She'd already begun pulling on her shorts. "I'm such a terrible person. Maybe I wanted to be with my boyfriend without him thinking of his precious motorcycle club for once."

She didn't get it. The Cobras were everything to me. As far as I was concerned, it was Cobras first, everything else second. I'd never told her otherwise.

When I did mention it, she rolled her eyes. And if she didn't understand, what the fuck was the point? "You're not my girlfriend," I spat out.

CULLEN

She was hooking her bra, but she suddenly stopped. I saw her face flame. But I'd never promised her anything. I didn't do girlfriends. Wasn't that for high school peckers? "Oh. Right," she said, as if she'd just forgotten.

I sat down next to her. "Look. You know what the club means to me."

"I do. But I also think I should mean something to you, too."

I'd frowned, grabbing hold of her slim shoulders. "You do. But I'm going to be the president. I have responsibilities." I'd been working toward becoming head of the club almost since day one. I'd never felt more honored in my life than the day I was named president of the Cobras. If one of the guys called me, there was no other choice than to be there, with them.

I'd checked my phone and reached for my jeans. "Look. I got to go. We can talk about this more when I get back."

She didn't say anything, just sat at the edge of the bed and looked at the ground.

I sat beside her and kissed her shoulder. "Come on. Don't give me shit."

"Me? I was close. And you . . ."

"That's to be continued, okay? I promise, you're first, when I get back."

She gave me a half-smile, and said, "I better be."

I'd left to go to the docks. I'd been there for the cargo shipment, and everything went smoothly. The guys probably could've handled it without me, but I knew if more stuff happened without me, they'd lose respect. So I shot the shit, went to The Wall and had some beers with them, carried on like it was any ordinary Friday night.

When I got back, it was sometime after midnight. Not rushing back, when I knew we were on thin ice? That was my second mistake.

My basement apartment was dark. And she was gone.

CULLEN

Not just gone from my house, gone from my life. She'd gradually moved more and more of her stuff from her grandmother's house over to my place, until she was pretty much living with me. But in the space of the few hours I was dealing with Cobra shit, she'd cleared it all out.

I looked everywhere for her. And she'd just disappeared.

Vanished into thin air.

And now, here she was, in my fucking guest room.

She'd left me before.

And now she was back. With a baby.

My baby.

And no fucking explanation.

I went to the bathroom and splashed cold water on my face. When I came back, I expected to see the kid in the bed. But she had her on the floor, on the plush carpeting, boxed in by pillows. "What? The bed not good enough for you?"

She shook her head and brushed a wisp platinum hair off the kid's forehead. "Ella tends to move around a lot. Don't want her falling off the bed."

Well. That made sense. When I last knew Grace, her job had been as companion for her grandmother, but since her grandmother was pretty with-it, that meant that all she did, day after day, was raid her grandmother's medical marijuana stash, sneak booze from her dead grandfather's liquor cabinet, and watch TV. She hadn't been a pillar of responsibility. It occurred to me that she had a lot more on her mind these days.

She turned down the lights lower and then followed me out to the hall.

I turned to her. "So?"

She looked hurt. "So what?"

"Dammit, Grace. I'm waiting. Are you going to explain to me why you left, and didn't tell me I had a kid?"

CULLEN

She just looked up at me, scraping her top teeth over her bottom lip in a way that made my cock twitch. It didn't fucking help that she was even hotter now. She hadn't been skinny before, but she'd filled out. Those curves were front-and-center, even in the oversize flannel shirt and cutoffs she was wearing. I didn't think it was homelessness that agreed with her; it was probably motherhood.

I tried to get my cock to remember that. There was a kid in the other room. My kid. And it was all my cock's fault.

"Well?"

She sighed. "Please don't be angry. It's been a really tiring night and—"

"So you're going to put me off again?"

Her eyes narrowed. "You're the one who was always putting me off."

She pushed past me and stalked down the hall, like she owned the place.

EVIE MONROE

There wasn't a single woman in this world who could get to me the way Grace Wilson could. She was infuriating. "Where the fuck are you going?"

"It's a big house. I'm going where I can be away from you until you calm yourself down and we can discuss this like reasonable adults."

I stalked over to her and wagged a finger in her face. "Baby, with you, ain't no such thing as reason."

Her face reddened, and her nostrils flared. "With me? Let's think back to the day I left you. Look me in the eye and tell me I was the one who'd lost her mind."

I pressed my lips together. Let out a laugh. Placed my hands on her cheeks, and gazed straight into her eyes. "You left me in the middle of the goddamn night. Without even a goodbye. You lost your fucking mind."

She tore my hands away from her face. "Yeah! Because you ran out on me first!"

"I. Told. You," I growled, my voice steadily rising. "I did that because. . ."

CULLEN

Suddenly I heard a wail. I stopped. Grace heard it too and shoved her palm into my shoulder. "Nice job, idiot," she said, rushing past me. "You woke her up. You really do have a way with kids, you know."

I shook my head and turned around, grasping handfuls of my hair. I sank to a crouch in the hallway, wondering if this was a nightmare. It felt like one. "Never signed up for this kid thing," I called after her.

She shushed me loudly as she went into the room.

I couldn't do this.

Couldn't take this.

Couldn't take her.

There was a reason we went our separate ways. She was stubborn as hell, and I didn't do relationships.

As far as I was concerned, I'd take care of the baby. Give her all the money she needed for the thing, and whatever she needed to get back on her feet. But I had my life. I liked my life. And nothing was going to get in the way of what I had.

EVIE MONROE

I stomped over to the room and was about to tell her that when she came out of the door. Her nose practically bumped against my chest, she was so close. She smelled damn good. And she was gorgeous. She looked up at me, waiting for me to speak.

But all I wanted to do was kiss her. Taste her.

Dammit. I was too tired to think clearly.

"I'm gonna go to bed," I muttered, turning away from her before my body could take action. "We'll talk about this in the morning."

I went into my bedroom and closed the door. I ran a shower to calm myself, and as I stepped into the warm water, I took my cock, pumping it, hard, in my fist. As I stroked, harder and harder and the hot steam swirled around me, I tried to think of a nameless face. Letting out a grunt, I pressed my forehead against the tiled wall and shot ropes of come all over the shower floor.

But no. I thought of Grace.

CULLEN

Fucking infuriating, incredible, gorgeous Grace, the only woman I'd ever felt anything for.

Fuck.

EVIE MONROE

CULLEN

Chapter Four

Grace

I woke up as the sun was poking into the blinds. I didn't have a phone, so I wasn't sure what time it was. For a moment, I forgot where I was, until I rolled over and saw Ella sitting up in her makeshift bed, sucking her thumb.

She was an early riser, so I guessed, six in the morning? That was about the time I woke up, too.

"Hey, baby," I said, crawling out of the bed and gathering her in my arms. "How are you, my little sprocket? You've been awfully good and quiet. Did you sleep well?"

She nodded a sleepy hello so I pulled her onto my bed and cuddled her a little, listening to her chatting and practicing her new words. Nose. Toes. Cheek. After we inventoried her anatomy, she struggled to be set free. First, I set her down on the floor and changed her diaper, which was heavy with pee. I picked through my backpack, looking to see if I had any more diapers. Only one left. Shit. I'd need to get to a store and stock up.

I hadn't gotten a good look at his neighborhood, but Cullen's house appeared to be at the top of a hill, a long winding drive away from civilization, including the nearest convenience store. I wasn't sure I could walk it with a toddler in tow, since I didn't have a stroller.

Hands on my hips, I looked at Ella, trying to decide what I was going to do.

She wasn't just sucking on her thumb, she was biting on it and whining. That meant she was hungry, and about to resort to cannibalism.

Okay. First things first. Find some food.

I scooped Ella up, groaning at how heavy she was becoming, put my hand on the doorknob, and nearly opened it when I remembered whose house I was in.

Dammit. I had to make sure I didn't look like the Night of the Living Dead.

CULLEN

I went to the dresser and looked at my reflection. Geez, and I thought I'd looked bad last night. My skin was sallow and I had bags under my eyes. I wasn't sure if that was from last night or the accumulation of a hundred sleepless nights, wherein my life had progressively turned to shit. I combed one hand through my hair and arranged my tank and boxers before stepping out of the room.

As I did, I remembered the way Cullen and I'd lie in bed together, sometimes until after lunch. He was a late riser and would always take afternoon shifts at the garage.

At first I thought, good. I don't need him.

But then I remembered I needed more diapers for Ella, and then I kind of did need him.

I set Ella down and together we padded into the kitchen. I opened up the refrigerator. Holy Code Blue. All he had in there was more beer.

Clenching my teeth, I looked at Ella. Things were so much easier when she was an infant and still breastfeeding. Now she wanted real food.

"Okay," I said, looking around. She tottered around as I rubbed my hands together, ready for action. "Plan B."

Shit. I really didn't have a Plan B.

I opened up the freezer and found a lot of ice. Then I looked inside the huge walk-in pantry and found . . . he'd converted it into a closet for all of his motorcycle gear? Really? Didn't this man eat?

Just then, Ella let out a shriek. I figured she was feeding off my desperation.

I started pulling open all the kitchen cabinets, willy-nilly, hoping for something. Cheerios. Didn't he eat Cheerios? Or what was he? A vampire? What the hell? No wonder his body looked so chiseled. He probably kept himself fed with pussy and motor oil.

Ella started to whimper, "Beckfist." If we were at the hotel, by now, I'd have gotten her breakfast. The

CULLEN

hotel had free continental breakfast, so I'd always filled up on bananas and cereal for her, sometimes a bagel and milk.

She was hungry. "Shh," I said to her gently, "We'll have *beckfist* soon, baby. I walked to the windows at the front of the house. Beyond Cullen's fortress of a stucco fence, I could see the road I'd come here on, curving dangerously downhill.

I went to the bottom of the sweeping curved staircase in the foyer and looked up. From here, I could see the door to Cullen's bedroom. Closed. He'd probably be in there for another few hours.

Then I looked at Ella, whose face was getting red. She let out a cry. I needed to make a decision, and fast.

"Okay, this is Plan B," I said to her, scooping her up and taking the steps two at a time. In the bedroom, I changed into my jean shorts and threw the flannel on, then, pocketing the hundreds Cullen gave me, went downstairs with Ella.

EVIE MONROE

I wasn't sure what I was looking for as I went around and opened the kitchen door to the garage. I stepped inside and saw two motorcycles; his, and another one I'd never seen. No car. Not that I had a car seat. Of course, no stroller. This wasn't Babies R Us. Oh, look, a wheelbarrow. That would probably get me taken in by Child Services.

I went back into the house to the front door. There was a keypad with an alarm system, blinking. I pressed the disable button, threw open the door and went out into the brilliant, sunshine-filled morning. Taking a deep breath, I settled Ella on my hip and walked down the winding path toward the street. She fussed at me to walk, but at the rate she meandered along, I didn't have time. "Let Mommy carry you, baby. You can walk later."

Even that short stretch had me out of breath. It wasn't just that I was out of shape—he just had a really long driveway. Damn him for living way up here, on this cliff side, instead of right next door to a Circle K.

CULLEN

I scanned down the hill. All I could see were the tile roofs of more houses. And a ton of trees. The houses weren't that close together. I guessed this was how the rich people lived in the hills. I had to do this. I took one step. And then another, patting Ella's back soothingly. I'd walked about a half a block when I heard a voice.

"Are you all right, miss?"

I looked over to see an old woman at the house next to Cullen's, crouching in front of a flower bed at the edge of the sidewalk, her gloved hands covered in dirt. "Yes, um—"

"You came from the McKnight house up the street?"

"I, uh . . ." I wasn't sure I wanted to lay claim to that. I could only imagine that the McKnight hell-raisers weren't the most decorous of neighbors. But I couldn't lie. "Yes."

I expected her to tell me to let Cullen know to keep the noise down. Instead, she stood up, wiped her gloved hands on her smock, and smiled at Ella, who was wriggling in my arms to get down. "What a darling."

"Thanks," I said, though she wasn't being very darling at the moment. "This is Ella. She's a little out of sorts right now."

"I'm Barry," she said, removing her glove and tickling Ella's chin. Ella looked at her, awestruck. "You're a cutie! She reminds me of my great-granddaughter. We watch her every day while our granddaughter's at school."

"Oh," I said, scanning down the street. I really needed to be on my way if I was going to get some food for Ella before she went into complete meltdown mode. And what if I went down there to the main road and couldn't find a convenience store nearby? Would I have to walk all the way back home, uphill?

Then suddenly, it hit me.

"Excuse me. I hate to trouble you, but do you happen to have anything for her to eat? Cullen doesn't have any food in the house. I have no idea when he'll get to the grocery store. She likes cereal or eggs, if you have any."

Barry looked thrilled. The little old lady with the gray hair even clapped her hands excitedly and bounced on the balls of her feet. "Oh. Of course! Bring her in!"

So that was how I ended up sitting on the outside deck of the Sumter's home, overlooking the ocean and feeding Ella a feast of fruit, cereal, and toast as Ella sat in the Sumter's high chair. Ella squealed and delighted us with her new words as we chatted.

I learned that the Sumter's didn't hate Cullen yet because they'd just moved in two weeks ago. "It's very nice to meet our new neighbors, finally," she said with a smile as she brought out a platter with fresh-squeezed orange juice and pancakes with real maple syrup for us to share.

"Actually, I don't live there, permanently," I explained. "I'm in between places right now. I'm just visiting Cullen. I got in late last night and didn't have a chance to do any shopping."

"Cullen? Is he the man with the loud motorcycle and the constant frown?"

I laughed as I stabbed a pancake. "That would be him."

"He doesn't look very happy," she remarked. "I've tried to be neighborly to him and he's been rather closed off. Is he upset about something?"

I nodded as I drenched my pancake in maple syrup. I hadn't eaten this well in ages. "Don't take it personally. He's like that with everyone."

Unless you ride a motorcycle or have big tits and red hair, he'll pretty much ignore you.

I ate about a dozen pancakes as Barry told me all about her life as a retiree. She'd come down from San Francisco with her husband, a retired lawyer. Her granddaughter had gotten pregnant in college, so now she worked during the days and went to school at night, and the Sumter's were helping to raise the child. She went on about how they were going to build a swing set in the backyard and how our kids could have playdates together.

I smiled, thinking. *Normalcy. That's just what Ella needs. This could be good.*

But I knew that wasn't going to happen. This was temporary.

When she asked me how long I was staying, I shrugged. I had no idea. I wanted forever. I wanted a place where I could lay down roots and be part of a community. I found myself feeling jealous of Barry's granddaughter, who had the real stability of a family to come home to. Even if the baby didn't have a father, she had love; so much love.

I was all Ella had. And really, Ella was all I had.

I tried not to think of that as I talked to Barry. We had such a nice time, chatting, that I didn't realize how late it was until I glanced over the block wall to the house down the hill a way, and saw the screen door slide open. This incredibly hot, muscular, tattooed man in nothing but boxer briefs stepped out, strode across the deck, and stretched as he gazed out at the ocean.

I watched him, momentarily dazed, feeling a tingling between my thighs.

Then I realized the person was Cullen. And wiped the drool from the corner of my mouth.

"Speak of the devil," Barry said, looking over at him. "He does know he has neighbors, doesn't he?"

You wouldn't think so, but as I knew well, Cullen was just a total exhibitionist. Hot as hell, and he knew it. Most of the time he was with me, he used to parade around his basement without a stitch. Barry was lucky he was wearing boxer briefs. I was pretty sure that eventually his new neighbors would wind up hating his guts, if not for his love of nakedness, then definitely for the loud parties, motorcycles, and every other hellraising thing that he did.

I stood up, stepped out from under the umbrella, and went to the railing. I cupped my hands around my

CULLEN

mouth, and shouted out, "Cullen!" as I waved both arms wildly.

He turned, raising his hand over his eyes to shield them from the sun. When he saw me, his lips curved into a grin. "There you are."

"Come over and meet your new neighbors!" I called out across the huge back yard.

He shook his head and mumbled something that sounded like, "Busy." Then he went back inside.

I snorted. The life of the party around anyone in his club, but a total asshole, otherwise. I frowned and turned to Barry. "I'm sorry. He's a little closed-off. But I had a great time. I really appreciate your help. And your helping Ella."

I went to lift her out of the high chair and noticed she was a little smelly. I cringed when I realized the first item on my shopping list had been diapers.

"Um, you wouldn't have any extra diapers, would you?"

Smiling, she packed up an entire plastic shopping bag with them. Enough to last another few days, at least. "Come visit again," she said. I thanked her over and over again, then went back to Cullen's house.

As I went in the front door, I heard the noise of a television down the hallway. I followed it and ended up in an actual cinema room, complete with a giant screen and rows of movie-theater chairs. Cullen was sitting in the very center aisle, watching a movie that looked very R-rated. To confirm that, someone spouted off a long string of curses, as I tried to shield Ella's ears. Then a woman took off her bra to reveal her enormous breasts. What a stirring epic.

Cullen watched, bare feet up on the seat in front of him, taking a swig of his beer. A beer? It was like, eleven in the morning.

Busy? My ass.

"You disabled my alarm?" he muttered.

I nodded.

He let out a low grumble.

CULLEN

"You missed the best pancakes," I said loudly, over a string of gunshots from the movie.

He didn't answer.

So I tried again, louder, "Are you ready to talk?"

He pointed the remote at me and pushed a button like he wanted to turn *me* off. He thrust his chin toward the screen. "I'm watching this."

I groaned, took the steps down to his seat, snatched the remote from him, and turned it off. The silence was miraculous. "Don't be an asshole. Let's talk."

He hitched a shoulder. "Why, baby? Didn't you get enough talking in with those people out there?"

Ella was wriggling, so I set her down to totter around my feet. "They're your neighbors. You could be nice to them."

He laughed, a low rumble. "I don't do nice, baby. You should know that about me by now."

I shrugged. "Well, I do. I didn't have anything for Ella to eat and she helped me. They're good people. So even if you don't do nice, it wouldn't hurt you to just wave at Barry, instead of looking at her like you want to kill her, since she saved your kid from starvation."

"*Barry?*" He said it like it was a curse. Then he shook his head. I don't think it had actually settled into his cranium yet that he had a child. A child that needed the help of adults, namely, her parents, for survival.

"Yes. That's her name. Barry Sumter. She's very nice. She's retired, and her husband is . . ."

"I don't care." He shook his head at me numbly.

"Okay. What *do* you care about?"

He sat up, laced his hands in front of him, like he was really listening. "Why the fuck you're here. Now. So go ahead. Talk. I'm all ears. Why did you leave me?"

I stared at him. He was giving me this superior gaze, like anything I said, he'd try to shoot down. He was in the Cullen Angry Asshole mood. When he got

CULLEN

that way, it was impossible to talk to him. "Because of that," I said softly.

He gave me a look, like he wasn't quite following. Then he laughed. "Because of what? Because I did something wrong, is that it? It's not you. It's never you. Just me?"

"Because I knew I was going to keep the baby. The second I found out I was pregnant, I knew I wanted it. And I almost did tell you, that day. But then, you got up, and left to go to your club, and . . ."

He stared at me, blankly. I wondered if he even remembered that day the way I did. He'd left so many women, since then.

"And I thought you'd tell me to get rid of it."

He crossed his arms. "Wouldn't have told you that. It's your baby."

"But she's your baby, too." I took another breath. "I knew the life you led wasn't the type of life I wanted for my child. And the person you were wasn't...wasn't..." I stammered. "Wasn't the type of person I'd want to be father of my child."

I watched his face carefully, waiting for the inevitable big reaction. I thought for sure there'd be one.

I thought he'd be pissed and yell at me.

Instead, the son of a bitch fucking smirked.

And then the smirk turned into long, low laughter. When he finished, he raised a palm to the ceiling.

"You got it. You're smart, baby. And right. If I were you, I wouldn't want me to be anywhere near that, either."

His eyes roved over to Ella. We could see her blonde head dashing between the seats, checking out the place like the energetic toddler she was.

"Would you stop calling her that? She's a she. And her name is Ella."

He rolled his eyes. "See? I'm a shit father." He sat up, taking his beer with him, and squeezed around me

CULLEN

in the seat, getting so close I could practically reach out and lick that tattoo on his chest.

I refrained. But I felt dizzy. I squelched the pang of need that hit me low in my abdomen. "I want her to have a father," I said. "Just not . . ."

He nodded. "Not me. Got it."

"No," I protested. "That's not . . . I'd want you, if you were . . ."

I saw the look in his eyes and trailed off. *If you were different.*

But finding out he was a dad wouldn't change this leopard's spots. He didn't want to change.

He climbed up the steps, then turned around, his ice-blue eyes piercing me straight to my core. His voice was low, growling. "Look. You can stay here as long as you want. My dad may have treated me like shit but he didn't back away from his responsibilities. I'll give you whatever money you want, on two conditions."

I nodded.

He came up close to me, so close that I could smell the hoppy smell of beer on his breath. His gaze traveled lazily over my face.

"One. You keep the kid out of my way. And two, you keep your tight little ass out of my way, you got that, mama? I love my life now, and I ain't gonna let either of you waltz in here and fuck shit up. Got it?"

I swallowed. And then I nodded, scooped Ella up, even though she kicked in protest. Wanted to run not walk everywhere. I took her back to our temporary bedroom, wondering how I could keep her in tow, my little live wire. How could we live under the same roof with him? I'd have to make it work. I didn't have a choice right now.

I wasn't sure what I wanted. For Cullen to suddenly become all mushy over the fruit of his loins and become father of the year? For him to profess his undying love for me? No, of course not. Maybe in a fairy tale.

But real life was far from a fairy tale.

CULLEN

Even though I'd been dreaming of the fairy tale ever since I was a little kid.

EVIE MONROE

Chapter Five

Cullen

Bullshit.

Bull fucking shit.

I sat there on my stool at The Wall, listening to the other Cobras drone on about their lives, trying to get into it. By then I'd had a six-pack and a few shots of Jack, but I was still a long way from being numbed to what had happened to me the night before.

She left me because she was pregnant and thought I was a fuck-up who'd fuck up her kid.

And yeah, she was probably right.

I was a fuck-up, family-wise, at least. Best left alone in the family department. Unlike my father, I *knew* it. I didn't profess to be a good dad and then go force my six-year old son to take a hit from my bong. I didn't promise to take my eight-year old kid to the beach and then get too sloppy drunk to do it. I didn't bring my eleven-year old kid to a poolside orgy so he could get his first blowjob.

No. That was my father.

As much as I cursed the DNA I'd gotten from him, I still had it inside me. I didn't trust myself, and no one else should've trusted me, either.

Drake sat next to me at the bar, hitting on a blonde with triple D tits, feeding her shots, and including me in the rounds he bought. So I kept knocking them back, one after the other, not saying much of anything.

"What the fuck is wrong with you?" Drake said. "You're being quiet. Is this a Fury thing?"

I shook my head, checked my phone. It was after eleven, so a good chance that my guests would be asleep. After she got done reaming me out about the kid not having anything to eat, I showed her this app where she could order anything she wanted and have it delivered. She'd placed the first order to the tune of $300.

CULLEN

I had no fucking clue how something that small could be that expensive.

I pushed off the bar and clapped Drake on the back. "You know, I'm gonna go home."

He gave me a bleary, heavy-lidded drunken gaze. Drake, our lightweight. "What? It's too early dude. You need to stay."

I shook my head, grabbed my helmet, and as I did, was cornered by a red-haired wet dream in a leather mini-skirt. "You're not leaving, are you Cullen?" she asked in a sultry voice that tugged at my cock.

She knew me, but I had no fucking idea if I'd ever seen her before. "Not unless I get to leave with you."

It didn't take long before she was on the back of my bike, and we were speeding toward my house. It wasn't my style to bring girls home from the bar; I usually went to their house. When they knew where I lived, they tended to show up at the wrong time.

But I didn't care about that, now.

EVIE MONROE

The house was dark when I got there. I pulled the motorcycle into the garage. The girl was all over me the second I stepped off the bike. The shots were starting to get to me. She wrapped her arms around me as I reached for the door to the house. "Hey, baby," I said, trying to disarm the alarm. "Give me a second."

I threw open the door to the house and she kissed me, wrapping her arms and legs around me. I walked her toward the living room, slowly unhooking her bra, until I remembered the furniture was all under tarps. Switching directions, I took her to the kitchen, where I sat her on top of the center island.

That's when I heard something.

A baby cried, so loud it sounded like it was coming from the same room.

I stopped. Removed my face from the girl's tits. Looked around.

"Don't mind me!" a voice sing-songed, as I saw her tear by me, a strawberry-blonde streak, on the way to the staircase.

CULLEN

Fuck my life.

"Hey!" I shouted after her.

"Who was that?" the girl asked, her eyes searching in the dark. "Was that a kid?"

I shook my head. "No one," I said, leaning in for a kiss. "Now where were we?"

She pulled away. "You're living with a girl? And a baby? Janice said you lived alone up here."

"Janice? Who the fuck is Janice? And that's no one. She's just staying for—"

Her squawk of a voice split my eardrums. "Oh, my God, Cullen. Is that *your* kid?"

She looked like she was going to laugh at me. I started to shake my head, as once again, my dick shriveled in my pants. Way to fucking ruin the mood.

I pushed away from her and vised my head in my hands. "Just get the fuck out?" I said, my voice just a breath.

Her eyes narrowed.

I reached for my phone. "I'll get you an Uber."

She reached for her purse. "No thanks, I'll walk," she said, a bitchy smirk on her face. "Can't wait to tell everyone that Cullen is a daddy. You'll make a great father, Cullen. Poor kid is gonna be so fucked up."

She didn't have to tell me that. I shrugged and plunged my hands into my jeans. "Just leave."

She opened the door and ran outside, laughing. "You're such a loser, Cullen."

I went to the center island and splayed my hands on it, staring at nothing for a long while. Then I walked to the foyer and started to climb the stairs up to my bedroom.

When I reached the top of the stairs, I sensed her presence at the end of the hallway, in the darkness.

I turned and saw her standing there, in a nightshirt, legs bare, her hair mussed and on her shoulders.

There was only one reason I'd brought that woman home to my house tonight.

CULLEN

Because I couldn't get Grace out of my head.

As long as she was here, I was too fucked up to do anything but think about her. Her pretty lips. Her perfect tits. The way she talked back to me with her smart mouth. The way she smelled. All of it, just down the fucking hall.

"I'm sorry," she said. "Ella woke up and was thirsty so I'd just gone down to—"

"Stop," I barked, reaching for the door handle. "I don't fucking care. I think I'm done with bitches for the night."

"I really am, Cullen," she said, sounding sincere. "I'm trying to stay out of your way. I didn't know that you'd be home this early."

I scowled at her. "You didn't know that I'd be home in my own house?"

"No. I thought you'd be out later, and Ella was—"

"Grace. I. Don't. Care," I bit out, pushing away from the door and stalking toward her. "You came back here because you needed money and a roof over your head. Don't expect anything else, because it's not happening."

"Have I asked for anything else?" she said, crossing her arms over her middle. For the first time I realized she was wearing just a nothing piece of t-shirt, all ripped and destroyed. Might've been one of mine. Her nipples were poking through the fabric. Hard.

Something in me must've snapped. I kept a close watch on my emotions, but only one woman could send them on a rollercoaster. And here she was.

I balled my fists and came up real close to her. "Not with your mouth," I said, dragging my eyes from hers, down to her hard nipples. I cupped one of her tits roughly through her shirt, to her surprise, but she didn't flinch away. I flicked the pad of my thumb over the nipple, making it harder yet. "With these."

She looked up at me, her breathing a deep rasp. "It'd be so easy for you, you know," she murmured.

I drank in those liquid crystal eyes, framed in thick, feathery lashes. "What?"

CULLEN

"To be the man your father never was."

I caged her between my forearms and said, "Not tonight. Don't fucking tell me what to do in my own goddamn house."

Then I bowed my head down and captured her mouth with mine. I kissed her savagely, brutally, angrily. Teeth and tongue. Biting and growling. I ground her against the wall as I clenched her tit in my hand. She let out a moan as I remembered just how good we were together. Just how fucking responsive she was. Our bodies fell in complete sync like cogs in a well-oiled machine.

The memory was my undoing, along with her, wrapping her hands around my neck, letting out a desperate sigh. She kissed deeper. Harder. All in.

When I pulled back, meeting her gaze, I realized she was shivering. "When was the last time you came?"

She gave me a stunned look, as if I was speaking another language. "I don't…"

"Wrong. It's now."

I flattened my body against hers, pinning her to the wall, feeling the soft curves of her. I ran my mouth relentlessly to her cheek, to her ear, down to her neck, and to her neckline. I groaned as I tasted her. I'd never tasted anything as good.

Breathless, she arched against me, clawing at my back. She let out a wanton little whimper, asking me to stop and begging me to keep going in the same breath as I reached under her t-shirt, wrenched a knee between her legs and spread her thighs.

She gasped as my fingers forced their way between her legs.

"That's it," I whispered on a hiss, rocking steadily against her. Watching her face because I wanted to see her come undone. I deserved that little bit of satisfaction, after what she'd done to me. I wanted to rip her apart the way she'd devoured me.

Her hands twisted in my hair, she breathed out little words, half formed. Pleading for more. My fingers climbed higher and higher.

CULLEN

My thumb eased against her panties. I rubbed the pad of my thumb back and forth over the silken fabric as I cupped her chin in the palm of my hand, hardly able to believe she was here, in front of me, after all this time. Grace. Fucking Grace.

I didn't want to fucking think. I just wanted to feel her under my hands, my mouth again.

I buried my face in her cleavage, rubbing my stubble against petal-soft skin as I worked the shirt up and kissed her perfect tits. I edged my finger under her panties and rubbed her clit. Then, no holds barred, I drove my fingers inside her. Pumping her hard, in and out, back and forth.

Her head dropped to my shoulder. Her mouth opened. Her breath came faster, in gasps.

She cried out as our shadows rocked back and forth on the wall, and her pussy clenched around my hand. Easy. She was so fucking easy to please. I stayed with her, milking her orgasm as she panted against me. It brought me right back to my sister's shit basement, where we'd fuck all night long, insatiably, bringing each other to orgasm after orgasm like animals in heat.

When I removed my hand and she straightened, she looked up at me, a stunned expression on her face, as I licked my fingers clean, tasting her. She was as good as I remembered, making me remember just what it was like to be an addict.

I'd inherited my addictive personality from my dad. He was addicted to it all: drugs, sex, alcohol, gambling. I'd flirted with all of those things, but then I'd stumbled upon the one habit that was more impossible to break than all of them combined.

This woman.

Grace.

And now, just like an addict, I was right back in the throes.

"Fuck," I muttered. I pushed off the wall, feeling that surge of adrenaline that comes before losing all control.

CULLEN

She blinked and said my name, hesitantly, as I lowered her shirt into place.

I turned and stormed into my bedroom, slamming the door behind me.

And for the second night in a row, I jacked off in the shower, thinking of her, and only her, as I came against the tile wall.

ature.

EVIE MONROE

CULLEN

Chapter Six

Grace

The following morning I woke, picked up Ella, and held her to my chest, shivering as I thought about Cullen.

I knew this would happen. I knew if I went to his house, I'd fall under his spell again. He was just too damn irresistible. Once he put his hands on me, I was powerless to stop myself from submitting to him.

Which was the reason why I put off contacting him until things became really dire and he ended up as my last resort. Really, if there'd been any other option, I would've taken it, if only to preserve my sanity.

Being in the same house with him, my sexy, infuriatingly hot ex with the hard body and penetrating eyes was a total recipe for disaster.

I couldn't sleep that night, after he'd put his hands on me and made me come, as easily as I breathed. He always had that magic touch where I was concerned—

all he had to do was call my name and I was his puppy; touch me and my body whirred to life.

As I cuddled Ella in bed, staring up at the ceiling, it was like I could almost feel those spider webs being wound around my body, pulling me to him. I'd escaped before, barely. I didn't know if I was strong enough to detach myself a second time.

I also felt something else, with even greater urgency: Incredibly horny.

Truth was, I'd had a few flings after Cullen, but they were nothing to write home about. Being pregnant wasn't the greatest way to find new guys, believe it or not. And having Ella, breastfeeding, and having my big fat post-baby body, had pretty much gobbled up all of my sex drive. So, when he'd asked me that question? About the last time I'd come?

It had been with him. Two years ago.

And last night? He'd awakened something inside me. Something feral, desperate.

CULLEN

Something that made me really afraid for myself, living in a house, alone, with him. I knew it was only a matter of time before I surrendered entirely.

I had to . . . I didn't know. Clear my head? Invest what little money I had in a vibrator? Anything to keep Cullen out of my head, and my pants.

It was early in the morning, so I felt safe going downstairs. I gave Ella some Cheerios and a banana from the huge delivery of food I'd ordered, and we sat down together in his cinema room to watch Dora the Explorer on the giant screen. For a minute, as Dora and Boots tromped all over God's creation, I thought, *maybe this could work. This house is huge. I'll just plan my days to make sure I'm never around when he is.*

And then I realized, as I deposited Ella the Explorer back in her seat for the hundredth time, that with a curious toddler in the house, staying confined to one area wasn't exactly easy.

Not to mention that part of me, a big part of me, really wanted Ella to know her father.

But not if he was going to be a dickwad, bringing women home and treating them like garbage. My dad had walked out on me when I was twelve. Been there, done that. Wouldn't want to subject my daughter to that kind of torture for anything in the world. It'd be better not to know her father than to feel that rejection.

After breakfast, I went over to the next-door neighbors and knocked on the door. Barry answered.

"Good morning!" I said when she answered with a bright smile. "I was wondering if you had a stroller I might borrow for a jaunt around the neighborhood?"

"Of course, of course!" she said, opening the door wide in a big welcome for Ella and me. "Wait here." She came back with a top-of-the-line jogger.

"Oh, thank you," I said, settling Ella inside. "I'll bring it right back."

She shook her head. "Keep it. Mariel bought it for me at a garage sale, to use with her daughter, but I never jog. We prefer the other stroller."

CULLEN

"Really? Amazing!" I reached over and gave her a hug. "You have no idea what this means to me. If there's anything I can do."

"Well," she said, walking us to the front of the house. "It's probably presumptuous for me to say, but . . . does your boyfriend have to ramp up his motorcycle late at night?"

"Oh." I knew this was coming. "He's not my boyfriend. But I could ask him to keep it down if he's coming in late."

"I'm sure it must've woken your baby, didn't it?"

Come to think of it, that made sense. Ella usually slept through the night, but something must've woken her. I'd been so deeply asleep I hadn't heard it, but that had to have been the reason she was up, and the reason we'd been downstairs when he'd stumbled in, drunk, with that woman. "I'll talk to him about it," I said.

And that'll go over like a lead balloon.

Ella waved at Barry. "Buh bye," she said sweetly, and Barry waved back. "Have fun, you two."

We went for a long walk, all up and down the hills of the development. I walked down to the edge of the development and found a Circle K not very far away. I also found a little park overlooking the ocean with a bench, and we sat there, just taking in the sun and sea air. It felt good, to be in a real, stable situation, for the first time ever.

Even though I knew the stability was short-lived, it still felt nice.

Then I went back to the house. I parked the stroller on the deck and went inside. King Cullen was up by then. I heard him in the cinema room, watching another R-rated epic.

I did my best to avoid him, but Ella was babbling, and he must have heard it. "Hey," he barked out as soon as I closed the door. "You disable the security system and leave here without locking the door again and I'll lock your ass out."

My jaw dropped. He did not just say that.

CULLEN

"Up, Mommy. Up!" Ella lifted her arms. I lifted her up with a huff and stormed into the room, just as an actor onscreen unleashed a barrage of curses.

I covered Ella's ears. "What did you just say to me?" I demanded.

Chewing on a toothpick, he didn't look up at me. "You heard me."

He was wearing just jeans again, his body draped out over the seat, his chest muscles and six-pack rippling in a way that was impossible to ignore. He wore a bandana wrapped around his head, which happened to be my favorite Cullen look. I willed my heart to be strong.

"No, I don't think I did," I snapped, putting my hand on my hip. "Because if you think you're going to lock me and Ella out of the house, you're mistaken."

He pressed his head against the backrest of the seat and looked up at the ceiling. "I think I'll do as I damn well please, baby, since this *is my fucking house.*" He growled the last part, and I felt Ella tense in my arms.

"You're an asshole," I hissed at him.

For the first time, he looked at Ella. He feigned shock. "Mommy's got a potty mouth. She's got to be more careful around you, precious."

Ella looked at him, lovestruck, and squealed in glee. Did she know her daddy? I hated how she was already wrapped around his finger, with just one sentence. He'd done the same damn thing to me. My fists clenched.

He flipped off the television, crossed his thick arms, and looked at me. "Sweetheart? Let's play a little guessing game. You know why the carpet in the living room is all ripped up? You know why there's fresh drywall on the walls? You know why I spent forty-thousand dollars on new windows?"

I stared at him. "What do you mean?"

He slid out of his seat and came up close to me, touching my cheek so that I flinched. "I'll let you come up with the answer. I promise you, it ain't gonna be one you like."

He moved past me, and I whirled to him. "Wait. Tell me."

He turned, leaned an elbow on the door jamb, near his ear, and shook his head in an infuriatingly slow way. "You probably ain't gonna want to take walks in this neighborhood anymore either, as long as you're living in this house. I don't got a lot of friends."

My blood went cold.

I thought back to some of the things he'd said to me about the Cobras. He wasn't able to talk much about the club, but once, a couple dudes had been shot, and he'd come home covered in his brothers' blood. Once, he'd nearly been arrested. And that was only in the few months we were dating. I told him if he was ever hoping to have a legit future with me, he'd need to get out.

He'd laughed at me at the time. But I thought, okay, as he got older, the Cobra stuff would get old.

He'd grow out of it. I didn't realize it was a lifetime commitment.

That meant that all those things he was so deep into, back when he was gunning for president of the Cobras . . . he was still into them. Maybe even deeper, now.

"You're president of the Cobras," I said. It wasn't a question.

He raised his eyebrows, like, *what did you expect?*

I guess what I'd hoped and what I expected were two different things. He was, what? Thirty, now? I'd hoped that by his third decade the gangster lifestyle would've lost whatever allure it held over him. But what had I expected?

I'd expected him to stay a Cobra as long as he lived. To die a Cobra, which would probably happen sooner than later, at the rate he was going.

I'd seen the way his eyes gleamed when he talked about the club. It was in his blood. Hell, he'd dropped me cold so many times because of club business. I'd never mean more to him than them. Never.

And neither would his daughter.

By the time this full realization had settled over me, he'd gone back into the kitchen. I trailed in after him, in a daze, and watched as he hunched in front of the fridge, and opened the gallon of milk, Ella's milk, and tossed it back. I watched him as he took long swallows, then wiped his mouth with the back of his hand.

"People shot at the house?" I asked, not sure I wanted to know the answer.

He looked over at me, a superior smile on his face, and said, "Shot? It was a regular wild west shootout, girl."

My stomach clenched. I looked at Ella. "Who?" I whispered.

He closed the refrigerator door and leaned against it. "You know."

EVIE MONROE

The tightness in my belly got worse. It was like everything from two years ago—his entire life—had been preserved and was an exact replica of the life he'd had before I left. The life I couldn't stand. Oh, the house might have been different, but everything else? The same.

"The Fury," I mumbled.

He nodded.

"Did anyone get hurt?"

He nodded again. "I always kept the alarm disabled for my guys. They came over the wall. I'm in the process of upgrading the system but they know where I live and they'll come again."

I swallowed.

"I told you, sweetheart. You don't want to have your name associated with me, if you can help it. I know what you're looking for. And you won't be happy here."

I sucked in a deep breath, then let it out. "Will you loan me some money? To stay in a hotel?"

CULLEN

Until when? What would happen then? Short of me winning the lottery or a fairy godmother appearing, nothing would save me.

He nodded, whipped out his big fat wallet and counted out ten one hundred dollar bills. "And take my number. Call me if you need more."

He scribbled his number down on a piece of paper and handed it to me, then told me he'd order me an Uber.

I folded the paper, put it in the back pocket of my jean shorts, and went upstairs to pack up our stuff to take Ella to someplace safe. As I climbed the stairs, I told myself this would be good. I didn't need to get myself or Ella entrenched in Cullen's chaotic life. Still, I couldn't shake the sadness that settled over me.

So much for finding a little bit of normalcy for Ella.

So much for the fairy tale.

EVIE MONROE

When I packed everything up, changed Ella, and started to lift her into my arms, I looked around the room, wishing to God I didn't have to leave.

Then I sank down onto the corner of the mattress, buried my head in my hands, and had a good, long cry.

Chapter Seven

Cullen

I left the house and set out on my bike, trying to convince myself I was doing the right thing, sending Grace away.

It *was* the right thing, for the life she wanted.

And for the life I wanted.

I didn't need myself to get entangled with her. The kid didn't need a shit father like me. Grace wanted us to play happy family, and that wasn't going to happen in my lifetime. If she thought we could do that with what I had going on with the Cobras, she was going to get us all killed.

So this was good.

Clean break.

I'd set up an account for her and arranged to have some money sent whenever she needed it. She could stay safe that way and take care of her kid.

EVIE MONROE

As I pulled into The Wall, I wondered why, then, it felt like something was gnawing away at me.

I went inside and ordered a beer. Saw Drake and Nix playing pool, so I sat down at a stool to watch them. The second Nix saw me, he made his shot, straightened, and came over to me.

"Where's your girl?" I asked him, giving him a fist-bump.

"Rehearsal," he said, taking a swig of his own beer. I remembered him saying she was a ballerina, which made me laugh every time I pictured him in the front row watching her. "So is it true?" he asked.

I raised an eyebrow as I watched Drake line up his next shot. "Probably not. What are we talking about?"

"Drake said Faith came in here late last night and started telling everyone you've got a kid."

I stared at him. Who the fuck was Faith? Then it came to me. That redhead with the annoying voice from last night. I frowned. "Yeah. Well, an old flame showed up out of nowhere a couple days ago, and she was staying at my house with her kid 'cause she's got nowhere to go. But she's leaving."

Nix rubbed the scruff on his jaw. "Good. We still don't know what the Fury's up to. After what happened a few weeks ago. If word got out you had a kid, they'd probably declare open season on the poor little thing."

I stiffened. "Just what did Faith tell people?"

He shrugged. "I wasn't here. But the Fury knows where you live. Wouldn't be hard for them to hit you where it hurts. You getting that security system upgrade?"

"It's in the works." Up until the shootout, the nine-foot wall around the perimeter had felt like enough. But after the Fury came to my home, I'd gotten quotes on an upgraded system with motion cameras and thought about employing armed guards. I'd come home a few times and gotten the distinct feeling my place was being watched.

What if they'd seen Grace and the kid?

I sat back in my stool, thinking. Fuck. If Hell's Fury knew about Grace, no place in Aveline Bay was safe for her. Especially some shithole hotel in town. They'd find her and hold her hostage the way they'd done with Olivia.

And I'd just sent her away, alone.

Shit, shit, shit.

I was jarred from my thoughts by Nix, snapping his fingers at me. "Yo. Did you hear me? I asked if you heard from Jet yet."

I shook my head.

"He and Hart said they got some intel on the Fury," he said. "We should meet tonight."

I nodded, paid for my beer, and stood up. "Yeah, we should. Church eight o'clock tonight."

"Yeah." He studied me. "You okay?"

"I don't know," I told him. "I've got something to do, first. I'll see you tonight."

CULLEN

I went outside, pulling my phone out of my pocket. Then I realized I didn't even have Grace's number—she had mine—and I had no clue what hotel she was going to. I stared at my phone for a few seconds, trying to think.

Then I searched a list of hotels in town and got down to work.

EVIE MONROE

CULLEN

Chapter Eight

Grace

I chose the Best Western Aveline Bay, a shabby little motel about a mile from Cullen's house.

At only fifty dollars a night, it wasn't in the nicest section of town. But it had a free continental breakfast and I figured I could stretch Cullen's money that way.

I settled Ella down in the rented playpen for her nap and set about filling the fridge with some of the items I'd taken from his house and organizing the cereals and dry foods in the kitchenette. Once that was done, I looked around the room, with its outdated furniture and boxy TV and wondered what the hell I was going to do next.

At the shelter, they'd told me I should apply for public assistance, which. They gave me a list of websites I needed to access. I'd have to use the computer at the public library, but of course, I'd have to wait until Ella woke up. I pulled out a newspaper I'd found in the lobby of the hotel and started to read through the Help Wanted ads. As if I could ever take a job paying minimum wage with a baby to watch.

As I was lying on my stomach on the bed, thinking this was hopeless, I was suddenly jarred by the loudest ringing of a phone I'd ever heard.

I jumped up, just as Ella started to wail.

Scooping up the receiver, I snapped, "Yeah?"

"Grace?"

It was Cullen.

I peered down at Ella and tucked her in, and she started sucking her thumb, nodding off again, thank God. I whispered, "What?"

"Great to hear from you, too, sweetheart." His voice was gruff. Sexy. Relaxed. After last night, it seemed now all he had to do was speak and I felt myself getting wet.

"What do you want, Cullen?" I hissed out.

"You, baby."

CULLEN

I gripped the receiver in my hand and fell back against the cushioned headboard. "Are you drunk?"

"No. But look. There's been a change of plans. I think you'd be safer either leaving town altogether or coming back to my place."

I straightened. "I'm not leaving," I spit out immediately. I'd never been anywhere but here. Going away, with Ella? That scared me more than anything. But for him to suggest it, something must've been happened. "What's going on?"

"Listen," he said. "Just sit tight there. You're at the Best Western?"

"Yes. Room two-ten."

"Geez, could you have picked someplace better than that shithole? Bad part of town over there."

"Didn't want you accusing me of wasting your money."

"I wouldn't do that."

"Oh yes, you would," I said with a bitter laugh. "You—"

"Hey, I don't want to argue. I'll be there later tonight. I got some stuff to do first."

And he hung up without so much as a goodbye.

I would've slammed the phone down on the hook if Ella hadn't been three feet away. Instead, I hung up quietly, stewing. *Go here. Do this. Sit. Beg.* He really did think women were his little puppies to command, didn't he? So now he wanted me back in his house, a house that had gotten ripped apart by bullets because of his association with his stupid motorcycle gang.

Gee, thanks for the offer, but no thanks.

And yet, as I sat there, thinking about the way he'd made me feel last night, I knew I was powerless to actually say that to him.

I looked down at sleeping Ella. "Don't let the way he talks to me fool you. Believe it or not," I whispered to her, "your daddy used to be quite the romantic."

CULLEN

My thoughts slipped to the past. Straddling the back of Cullen's bike, my arms wrapped around his strong back, that was where I felt safe. Protected, Loved. Once, we rode off together to the beach, my tits were pressed up against him. Every once in a while, I'd let my hands roam over his body. My hands, my fingers gliding over the bulge of his cock through his jeans.

We'd parked on the side of the road and hand in hand, made our way to a secluded cove that he used to go to when he was younger, where the sand was as white and fine as powder. He had pulled out a blanket that I hadn't known he'd brought. "You think you're getting lucky?" I'd asked him, surprised.

A corner of his mouth quirked up. "I'm already lucky, baby," he'd said. "I got you."

He'd spread out the blanket, and we watched the sunset, arms wrapped around each other. We'd kissed like no one else existed, with the seagulls crying out in the distance, the waves lapping at our bare feet.

Then, he slowly undressed me, worshipping my body, taking care with his explorations, licking each and every part of me, before he'd slowly entered me. Buried deep inside me, he'd whispered how much I'd meant to him, as he fisted the blanket and gazed into my eyes. "And you got me," he'd said. "You've always got me."

Growing up, I never believed much in love. My parents fought all the time. My dad walked out when I was twelve, and my mother, desperate for a man to love her, invited a string of total losers into our house, most of whom wound up hitting on me. I was raped by one of them, and when my mother found out, she was so beside herself with guilt that she killed herself. If love existed, it was meant for other people, not me.

But that night was the first night ever that I could see my future. The first night I had believed I could find love. That I could be Cinderella and live the fairy tale.

That night, I'd been so happy, I cried. Cullen asked me what was wrong, and I just moved closer to his naked body and told him that nothing could possibly be wrong. I had been crying because everything was so right.

CULLEN

And then . . . then it all fell apart.

All it took was a couple of weeks for that fairy tale to crumble. For the dreams I'd been amassing in my head to be torn apart. Cullen started spending more and more time with his gang, and some days, he didn't even come home.

I fell back against the pillow and stared at the ceiling. I wasn't sure I'd ever be able to trust Cullen completely again.

Not now.

I looked over at sleeping Ella, so sweet and angelic, her shriveled thumb at her little bow lips.

I had so much more to lose now.

EVIE MONROE

Chapter Nine

Cullen

Whenever I called church, I liked to be there early. I rode down the deserted pier, toward a setting sun, sinking beneath clouds. The massive white warehouse, once a place for storing shipping containers, loomed in the distance. As I approached, I saw two bikes already lined up outside.

I parked beside them and went in to the clubhouse.

The first thing I saw was Hart running his hands through his red hair. "Fuck me. Fuck me. Fuck me," he kept saying, over and over again as he paced the room. Jet was there as well, slumped on a chair, looking equally spooked.

"Dude. Thanks for the invitation, but I'll pass," I said, striding in and dropping my shit at the table in front of the room, where I usually sat when I conducted church. "What the fuck's going on?"

They looked at each other. Then Hart pulled out his laptop. Hart, our tech guy, had that laptop more attached to him than his own ass. He opened it and showed me a picture. I leaned forward, looking close at two men, who appeared to be in heavy discussion. "That's Bruiser from the Fury."

He nodded and pointed to the other guy. "That's Walsh."

Walsh dealt in stolen arms from overseas. "So they're buying up weapons."

Hart nodded. "A lot of weapons from the looks of it. I heard a couple of people online say that Bruiser's been getting in huge shipments. If those are guns, then they're prepping for an all-out war."

Just then, Drake and Nix showed up. I checked my phone. As usual, Zain was late. I paced the floor as Hart filled the other guys in. "So what does this mean?" Jet asked.

CULLEN

"It means just what we said," Nix grumbled. "That we should've wiped 'em off the face of the fucking earth when we had the chance."

I held out my hands. "Now hold on. Yeah. But look at it this way. They're building up their defenses probably because they expect us to go in there and rain hell on them."

Jet frowned. "They had another choice. They could've disbanded."

I shook my head. "After what happened last month, they still had more members than we did. They'd never just disband. Even without Blaze to lead them."

"But the point is, they're gathering strength," Drake said. "And we're the first targets they're gonna go after."

"No. Now listen. I don't know Slade like I knew Blaze," I said, hopping up onto the table and resting my hands on my knees. "But we still don't know what we're up against. Maybe Slade's just out to protect his guys."

Jet raised a doubtful eyebrow.

"Hell, it's what I'd do for you. If the Fury was on our asses, I'd make damned sure I'd built up our reserves to make sure they didn't try anything. That might be all Slade's trying to do."

Nix leaned back in his chair. "So what are you proposing? You proposing you meet with him?"

I nodded.

Zain walked in just then, as all four of the other guys were staring at me like I was insane. Zain frowned. "Shit. I missed something big again, didn't I?"

Drake hung his head. "Our esteemed leader is going to try to make nice with the enemy."

I shot Zane a hard look. "When I say eight, I mean eight. Not eight o five. Not eight thirty. Eight." I turned to Drake who looked surprised at my firmness. "Not make nice. But if we can avoid an all-out war, we ought to. I don't want to lose any of you. I don't want to put any of you guys in a bloodbath if I don't have to, got it?"

Nix nodded. "Makes sense."

CULLEN

Thank fuck I had him on my side. Now the rest of the club would agree. As I slipped off the table, it hit me. I'd have to somehow find a way to communicate with their new president. A guy I barely knew. What I knew of Slade was that he was from overseas and did a lot of travelling. He hadn't even been at the altercation last month. People called him cocky, smooth, elusive, quiet. Unlike, Blaze, he liked to fly under the radar.

"Hart," I said. "How do I get in front of him?"

"I don't think it's a good idea to do something face to face, Cullen," Hart warned. "He'd insist it be on his turf and it'd be too risky. I'll get a message to them that you want to have a call."

"All right. Do it soon. This can't wait. The sooner we put out these sparks, the sooner we can go back to the way things were," I said, thinking of Grace.

The way things were? It was funny how people never knew they were in the good old days until after they'd passed. I might never have had truly good days before, but when I thought about those months with Grace, I knew something for sure.

EVIE MONROE

That was as close as I'd ever gotten.

I checked my phone. It was after nine. I called an end to church, told the guys I'd see them later, and strode outside. The sun had already set, and the sea was a void of black as I straddled my bike and sped away from the docks.

I got to the Best Western motel after 9:30 and cursed at the piece of shit it was. A homeless guy wheeled a cart through the parking lot, and a group of gang-bangers were playing rap music at an ear-shattering volume in one of the rooms. I could hear their laughter and whoops over the roar of my bike when I pulled in.

"What the fuck," I said under my breath as I slid off my bike, eyeing those assholes. How could Grace pick this shithole?

I strained to see the numbers on the doors. All the bottom rooms started with a one. I found an outdoor staircase and climbed to the second floor.

CULLEN

On the landing, I saw a girl sitting alone, her bare knees pulled up to her chest, tangle of hair falling in her face. She was smoking a cigarette. When I got closer, I saw it was Grace. "For the first time ever, I didn't hear you coming," she said miserably.

"Hey," I said. "You shouldn't be out here."

"Don't got many places to go, it seems," she said softly, taking an uneasy drag of her cigarette. She blew the smoke out in a hard rush.

I walked up so that my boots were nearly touching her bare toes. "Didn't know you smoked."

She laughed bitterly. "I don't. But I really needed something."

She lifted the pack and offered it to me. I took one, tucking it in the breast pocket of my shirt. The whole building was shaking from the bass of the music playing downstairs. "No wonder. This place is shit."

She wiped her tired eyes with the back of her hand. Her fingernails were bloodied and chewed to the quick. Her pale skin trembled. "I'm tired. Ella won't go to sleep. She's in there right now, crying."

I listened but couldn't hear with all the other noise.

"All right." I reached for her. "You're coming with me, baby."

She yanked her arm away. "Like hell. I knew you didn't like me, but you want us to get shot to death?"

"I called the security company. I'm getting twenty-four-seven monitoring put in tomorrow. No one will be able to get in. I'll pick up anyone even hanging around the perimeter. You and the kid will be safer there."

She shook her head. "No, Cullen. You already showed me how much you want us in your house. Did something change?"

Just then, a car backfired. I broke into a crouch, my normal fight response, as Grace eyed me suspiciously. I exhaled and leaned over the railing to see the source of the noise just as whatever party was going on downstairs spilled down into the street. "Yeah. It changed. Word's been going around about you and the kid. If the Fury find out, they could come after you. That's why I want you where I can see you."

She shook her head slowly and rested her forehead on her knees. "Perfect. Just what I need," she mumbled. "As if I didn't have enough problems."

"And I can solve one of them, at least. Let me call you an Uber to get you back to the house. For tonight at least. You know you can't sleep here. We can talk about it more tomorrow."

There was a break in the music downstairs. I heard a baby's cry. She heard it, too, because she bristled. Then she stubbed out her cigarette on the concrete floor, pushed her back against the wall, and slid up to standing. "Fine."

I opened my phone and ordered the Uber, surprised at how quick she agreed. That told me that stubborn Grace had to be at the end of her rope. "On the way. Get your shit."

EVIE MONROE

She pushed open the door to the shithole hotel room and I peered inside. The sliver of light from the open door shone a light on a very red-faced kid with platinum ringlets. Grace lifted her up out of a playpen and said, "Can you help me?"

She went to hand me the kid but I backed away. Hell. Fucking. No.

"She's not a time bomb," she said, shooting me an incredulous look. "Fine. Could you get the groceries packed up and I'll get our bags together?"

I did as she asked, feeling stupid. She was right. It was a kid. *My* kid. What was I? A coward?

Ten minutes later, everything was loaded into the Uber and it was on the way to my house, carrying Grace and Ella. I followed on my bike, and by ten, we were inside. I flipped on the outside lights and armed the security system as she watched me, a sleepy kid drooping her head on Grace's shoulder.

"You're safe here," I told her.

CULLEN

She pressed her lips together. "Cullen. I don't know if we'll ever be safe, anywhere."

EVIE MONROE

CULLEN

Chapter Ten

Grace

After I got Ella settled into her bed, I tried to sleep. Ella fell asleep right away, but I ended up tossing and turning. When I did finally drop off, I had dreams of gunshots, and people running. Chaos. Ella screaming. Me running with her, trying to keep her safe, but falling, endlessly, into a dark hole with her in my arms.

I woke with a start, enveloped in that sinking feeling I got whenever Cullen would leave to be with his club and not return until much later than he said he would.

I rolled over in bed and looked at the ceiling. Strong morning light slashed through the blinds, painting prison bars above me. The irony of that wasn't lost on me.

But then I noticed something strange.

It was morning, possibly late morning, and Ella wasn't making her normal, nonsensical morning conversation with herself.

I cocked a sleepy eye toward her pillow fortress on the wall. Then I cranked my eyes wide open and flew up in bed.

Her makeshift crib was empty.

Wildly, I scanned the room. Her sweet blonde ringlets were nowhere to be found. I scrambled to the side of the bed and looked over. Opened the closet, finding it empty. Peered under the bed. Nothing.

Heart in my throat, I threw open the door and ran downstairs, nearly tripping as I grabbed the handrail and flung myself around it, toward the kitchen.

I smelled bacon at the same time I heard Ella cry out. I slid to a stop on the polished kitchen floor, hardly able to believe my eyes.

Cullen was standing in front of the stove, cradling Ella against his chest with one arm and holding a spatula in the other. Bacon and eggs were sizzling in a frying pan. He put the spatula down, cracked an egg on the side of the counter, and one-handed opened it and let it slink into the pan.

Wait. Cullen knew how to cook?

Ella wasn't crying in pain. She was smiling, big as ever, and observing the fledgling Gordon Ramsey's exploits with great interest.

When Ella saw me, she squealed in glee and started to kick her arms and legs in excitement. "Mama!"

"What are you doing?" I asked, rushing in and taking Ella away from the hot stove before she got splattered. My heart was beating double-time from the race downstairs.

"Relax, baby" he crooned in a low, sexy voice. "She and I were just getting to know each other. Making Mommy breakfast and shooting the shi—I mean, crap."

His eyes swept over me, and it was then I realized I'd fallen asleep in just a camisole and panties, the only clean things I had in my bag. Ella was running out of clean clothes, too. I really needed to do some laundry.

He licked his lips.

I knew that look. Knew that look well. Cullen always had sex on his mind. Always. He was a walking sex machine.

I felt naked. Bare, my nipples poking out.

I used Ella as my shield, holding her close to me and felt her diaper. It was swollen and bulky with pee. It was a good thing Ella never let a wet diaper get her down, but she probably had diaper rash by now. "She could've been splattered by grease. And her diaper needs changing."

He didn't look at me, just lifted the eggs and two slices of perfectly crisp bacon onto a plate with the spatula and said, "I think the words you were searching for are *thank you*."

I gave him a sour look. "For nearly killing her?"

"Relax. She was screaming. You were sleeping. I figured you needed your rest."

CULLEN

All right, all right. I was being too hard on him. Underneath all that bravado and motor oil, there was a good heart. He didn't know any better. And for once, he was thinking of someone other than himself. But after everything he was willing to put me and Ella through as a member of the Cobras, I wasn't about to let him get away so easily.

He set the plate down on the table and pointed at the chair. "Eat."

Once again, back to the dog commands. I thought of about a hundred not-so-nice comebacks for that, but I bit my tongue and went back upstairs to change Ella.

And of course, get changed myself. I slipped into a not-so-dirty pair of cut-offs and threw a hoodie on over my camisole.

When I came back, I felt a little more relaxed. In control.

Until I saw him sitting there, at the kitchen table, bare-chested and in his backwards base-ball cap, shoveling eggs into his mouth. He had a pile of mail in front of him and was reading a piece of it, oblivious to me gawking at him, thank God.

How was it possible or fair that he looked hotter, every day?

"Did Ella eat?" I asked him dubiously, sitting in front of my plate and setting her down on my lap.

"Banana," he said with a nod. "Didn't know what else you gave her."

I saw that her sippy cup had been filled with fresh milk. She reached for it and started to suck on the mouthpiece happily. I broke off a piece of bacon and shoved it in my mouth.

It was divine.

I finished off my breakfast in record time. You'd think I'd never eaten before in my life, for the way I devoured it. But no, it was just that good.

"I thought you didn't wake up until after noon," I said to him.

He shrugged. "Told you. The security people came to start the installation. We're gonna make this place a fortress, just you watch. A regular Alamo."

"Oh?" I looked around. I hadn't noticed that anything was different. "And that's going to make Ella and me safe?"

He nodded. "That and my men."

"Your men?" My skin crawled. Those Goddamn Cobras, who he could never forget for a second. "When are you going to see that they're the ones who got you into this situation of needing added security in the first place?"

He set down the piece of mail he was looking at and gave me a hard glare. "Grace. Maybe it was touch and go before. But I'm president now. They ain't gonna let anything happen to me or my people. That includes you. You're safer than the President of the fucking United States here. Okay?"

"I don't understand. The Fury will be after me just because I know you? They hate you that much?"

"I don't know what they'll do."

"So anyone who knows you is in trouble? What about Aria?"

"She moved to New York a year ago with her boyfriend."

I looked at Ella and inhaled sharply. "This isn't the kind of life I want for Ella. Gunfights? Feuds with other bikers? Not knowing whether her daddy's going to come home from one day to the next? It's not good."

He exhaled. "All right. Then I won't get too close to her. Is that what you want?"

Ella was gazing at him, her eyes drooping closed. It was time for her morning nap, I guessed, but the way she was looking at him? He'd already gotten too close. The fortress and security cameras outside could only do so much. I needed to put a wall around our hearts, too.

I'd been there. I feared that kind of damage could be a lot more severe.

"Yes," I said. "That's what I want."

CULLEN

It didn't seem to break his heart. He bit down on a piece of toast and started to read his mail again. I loaded my dishes into the dishwasher and settled Ella down for her nap. When I stepped out of the guest room, I heard a shower running somewhere.

As I walked to the stairs, I heard the shower turn off. I noticed the door to his bedroom was open, for the first time. I peered in and saw a massive, dark mahogany four-poster bed, like something royalty would have, covered in a pile of rumpled blood red sheets.

I wondered how many women he'd entertained between those sheets.

As I was about to move away, the door to the master bathroom opened, and he slipped out, wearing nothing but the tiniest of towels, wrapped dangerously around his hips.

I'd always known that Cullen was glorious in the body department. Even two years ago, he had the six-pack, the bulging pectorals and corded muscles on his arms. The snake tattoo on his stomach was his first tattoo, he'd gotten it on a dare when he was eighteen. But now? He was covered in the most delicious ink. Everywhere. And everything just seemed more chiseled. More cut. More tanned. More *man*. He was six feet of pure, hard, inked beauty.

I froze when he caught sight of me. A thin, devilish smile spread over his lips. "See something you like, baby?"

I opened my mouth to say no, but nothing came out. Because HELL YES. All of it.

Still grinning, he reached to his hip, loosened the towel, and let it fall.

"How 'bout now?"

His cock. Oh, my God, he had an amazing cock. And it was there, only semi-hard but hanging proudly between his legs, saying "here I am!" like it knew it was something special.

And yes. I wanted it.

Even more now.

CULLEN

So much more now. Warning bells went off, but I ignored them.

I felt wetness between my legs and my salivary glands kicking in at the same time. An aching need, low in my abdomen, gripped me.

He knew it, the cocky bastard. He'd always had a shit-ton of confidence, but now as Cobras President and owner of the nicest house in Aveline Bay, he was even worse. He was just taunting me.

Oh, fuck him.

No . . . hell no. That was the last thing I needed.

I lifted my chin and forced myself to turn away. "Nope. Get some clothes on, cowboy," I called back, running down the stairs and hoping the image of his beautiful body wouldn't remain embedded in my brain.

He called back, "Damn!" and I heard him rolling back his closet door. I had to smile at that.

I went into the kitchen and looked at the pile of mail he'd been reading. I didn't want to snoop, but I ended up looking at a checking account statement that had so many zeroes in it, I had to count them up. I squinted as I realized that he'd withdrawn forty-thousand dollars from the account, last month, *alone*.

Damn. I knew Cullen liked to flaunt his cash like a pimp, but I wondered if any of that money was spent wisely, or if it was all spent on things like beer, parties, women and his guys.

Frowning, I went to the fridge and poured myself a glass of ice water just as he came down the stairs. He was wearing jeans and a tight black t-shirt, the sleeves so tight around his biceps I thought they might pop out.

He looked delicious, as usual.

I thought he might go back to his cinema room and start watching inappropriate movies, but instead, he leaned against the counter and said, "So you slept well last night?"

I nodded. "It was better than the Best Western. Much better than the shelter. So I guess I should thank you."

CULLEN

He raised an eyebrow. "But you won't. So you're telling me the shelter was worse than the shithole you were in last night?"

I took a drink from my glass. "Well, at first it was okay. A bunch of women lived there, and they volunteered to watch Ella while I looked for work. But then they moved on and these men moved in. It was supposed to be a women's shelter but somehow, they started letting these guys in. And I was too scared to sleep at night. Too scared for Ella. I don't think I slept at all, the whole time. I knew I had to get out. Which is why I came here."

He stared at me, eyes dark, shaking his head. "Fuck, girl."

I gave him a get-real look. "We can't all live in multi-million-dollar mansions on the ocean, Cullen."

"All right. But there are other choices, girl. I can't believe you even thought to take her there."

"So she's a her now? Not an it?" I said with mock surprise, slumping against the refrigerator. "This is what I'm telling you, Cullen. I didn't have a choice."

He crossed his arms. "You did. If I knew, I would've helped you."

I stifled a bitter laugh. "Sure you would've. Which is why you fought me tooth and nail when I first came here and wanted to stay?"

His eyes darkened on mine. "Things are different now."

I snorted. So he was going to lecture me about how to take care of our child, when he didn't even know how to change a diaper? My anger was rising, and I knew I had to get away. I started to retreat, but curiosity got the best of me. "Oh? How?"

"Because of this," he breathed.

He bridged the distance in half a second and crushed his mouth onto mine.

Chapter Eleven

Cullen

I kissed her, devouring her mouth like she was my last meal.

I knew I shouldn't be doing it but then again, nothing had ever felt so right. I was in too deep but I'd be damned if I was going to turn back now.

I should've known it from the first time. Her body, her kiss, the way she moved against me . . . it ruined me for all other women. I was hers. She was mine. Nothing else would ever make sense.

And the only thing that had changed?

I accepted it.

Accepted I couldn't get her out of my head, no matter how hard I tried or how much time passed. I needed to sate this thirst once and for all, fuck her out of my system.

She broke the kiss and led me up to my bedroom. I kept my hands on her waist, under her sweatshirt. Fucking delirious.

There we were, back in sync again. She must have wanted to fuck me out of her system, too.

We already knew that plan had doom written all over it. But nothing was going to stop us now. I wanted to enjoy this moment, this sweet and fucking hot as hell moment.

The sun streamed in through the blinds, giving me a good look at the desire in her eyes as I dragged her closer. She came to me willingly, and I slid my hands under her ass, lifting her up so that her legs wrapped around me. Her lips met mine and she guided the kiss, her mouth parting and welcoming my tongue as her sexy little body rocked against mine.

"Fuck me like you used to," she begged me. "Just like that."

My brain spun like a top. Grace, wrapped around me, wanting me, kissing me like a maniac. Grace. Like

CULLEN

I hadn't thought of her a million times since she'd left. I wanted to make love to her and fuck her at the same time. I wanted her to scream in pleasure and rue the day she ever walked out.

I scooped her up and carried her to the bed. "I plan to, baby."

I laid her down on my rumpled sheets and stripped off my t-shirt, her greedy little eyes scraping over each and every one of my muscles. Her strawberry-blonde hair fanned out on my mattress.

I smirked down at her as I yanked at those barely-there shorts, pulling them over her wide hips and perfect legs to reveal a slip of pink lace underwear. Pulled them down, too.

Propped her legs on my shoulders and dove in, lapping hungrily at her cunt, dying to get her trembling under my touch. To get her as riled up as I already felt. She was already wet as hell, so fucking sweet.

I ran my hands up her abdomen, cupping and squeezing her tits as she moaned and wriggled.

Her hands found my face, dragging me forward. When I was close enough, she yanked hard on my belt buckle. "Just fuck me. I'm so ready for you."

I wanted it. Hell, I wanted it more than anything. But fuck, if I did that, it'd be over too soon. I parted her legs and settling my hips between them. She shivered as I dragged the tip of my tongue across her nipple. Slow, licking in circles. She canted her body toward me, wanting me, waiting for me to thrust inside her, take her. Ravage her. Savagely fuck her and own her the way she owned me every one of those nights she'd left me alone.

I sucked her nipple, rolling my tongue against her soft flesh as I eased a finger inside her, my cock hard as a fucking rock wanting to take its place. I loved the way her quivering walls closed around my finger as she let me take her a little bit at a time.

If I rushed, I knew I'd lose it. I'd waited too long to get here, and I was going to make it last.

I fingered her clit again, lapping at her nipples. I needed to make sure she was hot and ready because I knew once I was inside her, I wasn't going to last. This was too good.

I eased back to jerk off my jeans and boxers, then I crawled back over her, wanting her hands on me.

"Cullen." She blinked up at me as if she was seeing all of me for the first time. Her hand came up to my jaw and she just stared up at me with a look of admiration that made me think I could be the man she wanted me to be.

It did a number on my head.

I wanted it slow. Wanted to take my time and make it last.

But my body wanted other things. I reached into the bedside table, yanked out a condom, tore it open and rolled it on my dick. Then, I grabbed hold of her hip, and eased my cock to her entrance. She watched me, her teeth raking over her bottom lip. "Now," she begged.

Not so easy. Too soon and I'd lose control.

I focused hard on keeping it slow, rolling my hips into her until I was buried to the hilt. Connected. And Goddamn, it was better than I remembered. Hot, wet fucking paradise. I wasn't going to last, even being still like this. I felt the blood rushing hard through my veins.

She gasped and rocked into me, wanting me to go harder, faster. But I couldn't.

I breathed a shushing noise into her ear, lifting both her hands and pinning them onto the mattress, above her.

Palm to palm, body to body, locked together, the heat of her perfect body under mine was enough to make me go crazy.

There was no other choice. I had to move. Feel her. Feel more of her.

I started to, slow at first. In, out, feeling as much as I could of her, getting a rhythm. "Like that?"

CULLEN

Her breath hitched as she rocked into me, wrapping her legs tight around my waist. "Yes, right there."

Rolled deeper. "Good?" Got into a groove.

Her fingers tightened on my ass, pulling me into her. "Yeah. Oh, fuck, Cullen. Yes. Just like that."

I slowed myself down, pulled onto my knees, got her onto my lap. She arched her back and closed her eyes. Gripped handfuls of the sheets, lifted her chin back so I sucked on her pale neck, rolling her nipples between my fingers.

Rocked harder, further. Deeper. Holy shit, this woman was pushing every one of my buttons. I knew it, but only right now did it hit me how fucking perfect our bodies fit together.

Found myself getting too wound up too soon. Not where I wanted to go just yet. Steadied. Bit my tongue.

Knew it was no fucking use. Grace was too hot, too beautiful and this was too good. She started to grind on me, finding her own rhythm, so I met her movements with a strong thrust, which was just enough to push her over the top.

I set her off with a scream. "Yes. Fucking yes," she ground out as I grabbed her hips hard, jerked forward and unloaded. It was too fucking amazing, as fucking Grace always was. I just kept coming and coming and coming.

I slipped her off of my lap and collapsed next to her, sweaty and out of breath, and pressed a kiss into her bare shoulder.

She lay there for a minute, her tits heaving with each breath, looking well fucked and rightly stunned. Like she didn't know this would happen?

She belonged with me. That was it. No question.

She started to get up and I nudged her down. "Where do you think you're going?"

"We were pretty loud. I've got to make sure Ella is okay," she said, smoothing her hair and looking around for her clothes.

CULLEN

"Stay here," I told her, standing. "I will. I've got you right where I want you. You're not getting out of my bed without going through me first."

She rolled over and looked at me. "Put something on first!" she said when I reached the door.

I bent over and scooped up my boxer briefs and stepped into them. "Happy?"

She nodded. I went across the hall, opened the door a peek. The kid was still sound asleep.

I went back to my bedroom and slid the boxers off, then crawled back into the bed.

"She's out, girl. Get your ass over here. I'm not done with you yet."

EVIE MONROE

CULLEN

Chapter Twelve

Grace

"Tell me something, baby," Cullen growled as I curled up next to him with my head on his chest. "When you left that night, where'd you go?"

I sighed. I didn't want to think about it. "Does it matter?"

He nodded. "I'm asking because it was night, you were pregnant, and damned if that didn't take some balls. You must've really hated me."

He was right. Nobody could get me as pissed off as Cullen McKnight could. I rolled onto him, kissing his chest. "Yeah. So?"

"So next time you're thinking of skipping out on me, tell me. We'll have a talk. Okay?"

I gazed at him, not willing to answer that. It all depended on how much of an asshole he was.

He played with my hair, threading it through his fingers, which were stained in motor oil. He had that delicious smell of badass and motor oil that made my knees week. "You have any boyfriends since me?"

I raised an eyebrow. "Oh. Tons. Being pregnant is a definite man magnet."

He shrugged, tracing a finger up my spine, to the only tattoo I'd ever gotten, a cluster of birds, flying away, from my collarbone to behind my ear. I'd gotten it with him, on a dare, I think when we were a little drunk. It was hilarious, now, considering I'd flown away from him, and how I never flew, really. I'd left him, but was always nearby, in Aveline Bay. Maybe part of me had always been hoping he'd find me.

"You're hotter now, baby. Even as a mom. That body of yours . . . fuck. I didn't think it could get any better. I want to keep you in my bed and fuck you well and good. I bet all the other men did, too."

I laughed. "You sound jealous."

"I am."

CULLEN

I just smiled at him. "Jealous of no one. They didn't exist."

"They exist. You just didn't know it. But you belong to me, baby. And I'm not going to let anyone touch a hair on your head."

It was early afternoon, so I wasn't sleeping anyway. But now I really wasn't sleeping.

As I lay in Cullen's arms, wondering how the hell I'd gotten the strength to leave him before, it gradually settled on me. Things weren't different.

And I'd just gone and made them a hell of a lot more complicated.

But the funny thing was, I didn't care. My life had always been complicated. Maybe this was just made to happen. Why else was I never able to forget him?

I knew I'd be safe with Cullen. I knew he'd die to protect me. And Ella, too, though he hadn't warmed up to her yet. She'd wrap him around her finger. Soon. And though it wasn't the life I would've chosen for her, I wanted her to know her daddy.

We could be happy together.

I told myself that, again and again, as I held him tight.

Then I heard a cry. Ella was awake.

I expected Cullen to keep dozing, or pretend not to hear, but he slipped out from my arms and kissed my forehead. "I'll get her. You stay there."

I sat up on both elbows and looked at him. "You sure?"

He nodded as he slipped into his boxers and jeans. "I'm not helpless. I got this."

I smiled. *This I got to see.*

Curiosity got the better of me about three seconds after he disappeared out the door. I threw on his t-shirt and crept into the hallway.

He was already cradling a babbling, grinning Ella in his arms, bouncing her like a true pro. "Hey, kid," he said in a low voice. "Where's the fire?"

CULLEN

No wonder she was grinning madly at him. There could be no hotter sight than this.

He motioned me toward the bedroom. I went back inside and he brought Ella in, and put her down on the bed. She rolled around onto her hands and knees and looked around at the pillows. He sat down on the side of the bed, and I thought, *oh, gosh, we are such a cute little family.*

Then I looked over and saw his leather *kutte* hanging on the back of the door, with the Steel Cobras crest on the back.

Suddenly, I was back on the foldout couch in the basement of his sister's house. It was after midnight, and Cullen had gone to church and said he'd be back by ten.

That was when I flipped on the television and saw the local news reports of a shootout out by the docks, right where Cullen said the Cobras met. He'd gone out, shoving his gun into the back of his jeans, all badass, saying that some guys were trying to fuck with them and he needed to represent and show them who was boss.

When he'd returned, that vest of his was covered in blood. It bled through his fingers and the tiny handkerchief he'd put over it, dripping all over the floor. The second I saw him, I shrieked. I thought he was dying.

But he was lucky. A bullet had grazed his chin, coming just inches away from his artery in his neck. He still had the scar, a tiny white nick buried somewhere under all that beard. He'd told me, as we lay in bed that night once the bleeding had stopped, that he'd been getting out of church and some gang members had just opened fire on them. He wasn't sure who they were, or why they were after him, but, "Baby, what can I say? We got a lot of enemies."

A lot of enemies.

So many enemies, he didn't even know who they were. How could he protect me when he wasn't even sure where the danger was coming from? How could we be a family like that?

CULLEN

I looked around as Ella innocently explored the bed, rolling around the pillows. Somewhere, in this room, I bet Cullen had a gun. Loaded. He was always stupid and dangerous with it. He'd leave it lying around, loaded, anywhere.

If things were going to work, we'd have to baby-proof this house. First rule: Locking up all the guns. Because there was no way in hell he'd ever leave the Cobras. So he'd always have those enemies.

I reached over and felt her butt. "She needs her diaper changed."

He quickly handed her over to me. "That's where you come in."

"Oh, so, you don't want to learn?"

"Hell no," he said, shaking his head. "She's a girl."

I took her into the other room and spread her out on a blanket on the carpet. Her diaper was bloated with pee. I peeled it off as he averted his eyes. So now he gets a sense of shame? Oh, boy. I said, "Hand me those wipes and a diaper."

He looked at the assortment of things on the dresser and finally found the tub and a diaper, which he handed to me. I lifted her legs with one hand, and then she started kicking, twisting and screeching for Cullen. She might have been sweet as pie with him, casting his hypnotic spell to quiet her down. With me, she was her bouncy, toddler, lightning-in-a-bottle self.

I couldn't get her to stay still long enough to change her diaper.

"You want to help?" I asked him, grabbing her before she scrambled off the bed. "Well help me calm her down."

So he came over to the bed and sat down and did some trick with his fingers and she stared as if hypnotized while I did my thing changing her.

"There," I said as I finally put her bloomers into place. "Easy when we're a team. Thanks for your help."

He was still averting his eyes from the diaper part of the operation, focusing on the broad smile and chorus of giggles he had coaxed out of her. "I'm glad. But I ain't ever doing that."

Hmph, I thought, giving Ella the sign that she was free. She cooed happily and peeled off the bed, ready for action again. I handed her a sippy cup of water and she drained it, giving him her big blue eyes.

"Never say never."

He leaned against the wall and plunged his hands into his pockets. "Read my lips, baby. NEVER."

Right. Cullen was too damn stubborn. All in for fun and games but try to find him when it was time to go to work. "Fine." I stood up and started to chase her as she ran past him for the door.

"Where you going?"

I started toward the staircase. "You can't keep me in your bed forever, Cullen. I've got our daughter to take care of now. And right now, she wants to play and have a little something to eat." I managed to catch her hand and kissed her petal-soft skin. "Don't you baby?"

EVIE MONROE

Her answer was to wrestle herself away from me and follow her daddy around like a cute little puppy looking for treats.

In the kitchen I looked around at all the beer and liquor bottles on the shelves and decided that today, I'd work on tossing them out. If he wanted to keep me here, I was going to make the place safer. I fixed Ella her lunch and sat her on a high stool with a back at the counter. As she stuffed her little rosebud mouth, I started making a list of things we needed to baby-proof.

Cullen walked into the kitchen a few minutes later, so I ripped my list off the pad and handed it to him. "Can you get this for us? Maybe at Target? They have an aisle just for baby safety stuff, so it shouldn't be too hard to find."

He read it over. I expected him to argue. As he usually did. Instead, he nodded. "What the hell is a tot-lock?" he asked.

"It keeps cabinets closed so that a baby can't get into them and drink anything dangerous."

CULLEN

"I keep my alcohol up high."

I rolled my eyes at him. "Not that. Cleaning products. The stuff you keep under the sink."

He narrowed his eyes. "I don't have any cleaning products."

I looked around. "Obviously. So you never clean this place?"

"I have a housecleaning service come in. Once a week."

I looked at all the beer bottles and scoffed. "Did she miss a week or two? And obviously, you're not used to kids. Not that I'd expect you to be, but can we do it more often than that? With a toddler, things get pretty messy, pretty quick."

He gave me a look like I was speaking a foreign language, but as I stared at the list in his hands, I figured that was good enough for a start. We'd already upended his whole life. I didn't want to freak him out completely.

Before he left, he activated the security system, kissed us goodbye, and then I took Ella on a tour of the house, trying to find something to keep her occupied. Cullen's mansion was so huge, there were rooms I didn't think he ever used. This would probably be great for hide-and-seek games next year when Ella was a little older, but I didn't see many things around that were safe and fun for her now.

I wondered where he kept his gun. Knowing Cullen, if he was out with his guys, he probably had it with him. I kept Ella distracted on the other side of the bed and sure enough, when I peeked in the drawer of his night-table, I found a never-ending stash of condoms and a few loose bullets, rolling around there. But no gun. I would have freaked if I'd seen one with Ella so close. I just breathed a sigh of relief and we continued our tour of the house.

The next room I chose had a wall of framed platinum records, all belonging to Cullen's dad. There was even an old guitar hanging on the wall alongside a picture of a balding, longhaired man that I knew was

CULLEN

Cullen's dad. He was balancing a smiling boy with a bowl haircut on his knee who couldn't have been much older than Ella.

Cullen.

I thought back to the one and only time I met Brent McKnight, the rock-star legend from the heavy metal band The Fritz. When I met him, he was sitting in Aria's house, drinking beers with like six empty bottles lined up in front of him and Cullen.

Although he was almost bald on top, his mane of long, stringy hair hung like a dirty curtain around the side and down his back. Despite his skinny arms and legs, he had a beer belly and his ruddy face showed his love of booze. He'd brought along a girlfriend who didn't even look legal; she had some track marks on her arms, as did he. The tension in the room was so thick, I could tell Cullen and Aria didn't want him there.

When he'd looked me up and down, I could *almost* see a resemblance to Cullen in his blue eyes, though they were glazed from whatever drugs he'd been doing that day. He'd fastened those eyes on my cleavage and said, "What do you see in that fucking pussy boy of mine? Sit that cute little ass of yours on my face and I'll show you what a real man can do."

Really. A class act.

And his girlfriend hadn't batted an eyelash. I'd felt so sick after that I went to the bathroom and retched over the toilet for a good ten minutes. And I wasn't even pregnant yet.

All I knew was that if Cullen ever thought of treating me like that, I wouldn't just leave him. I'd kick him repeatedly in the balls first. Hard.

I knew he hated his dad. But he never said much else. I guess he didn't hate him enough to toss all this stuff away. His father wasn't a good dad. I figured Cullen must've wrestled with that, every day. *Would he be like his father?*

Ella was his chance to find out.

I knew it scared him.

And Cullen didn't like to admit anything scared him.

CULLEN

But I bet it scared him even more than the thought of taking a bullet from the Fury. He may have talked a good game, like he didn't give a shit about anyone or anything else, but some things he'd easily defend, paying no regard to his own safety. The Cobras. Me.

Maybe one day, Ella as well.

I went through a formal dining room, complete with a glass table that Cullen had probably never used.

Then we made it down the hall and went through about ten more giant, dark rooms that didn't have any furniture. I wondered why he hadn't sold this place, when I knew there was no nostalgia attached to it, and it was clear he didn't need all the space.

He had a nice swimming pool, though, with grottos and waterfalls and a hot tub. I could imagine teaching Ella to swim there. There was also a little pool house, butted up against the edge of the property, that probably had an even better view of the ocean. Cullen had told me he'd stayed there as a teen, when his father's partying had started to get out of hand. I slid open the screen door and started to walk outside, to the deck, but then I worried that would set off the alarm.

When the phone in the kitchen started to ring, I debated if I should answer it. I finally picked it up.

"Hey," a voice said right away. It was Cullen. "You got the code to disarm the alarm? There's a delivery truck coming, and you'll need to let them in."

"Yeah, I got it. You sent a delivery truck?" I asked. I was pretty sure my list wasn't all that long. Of course, he only had a motorcycle, so that made sense.

He hung up and when the delivery truck arrived about a half hour later, I disarmed the alarm and opened the door, expecting a few big bags. But the man in the red uniform was holding a massive teddy bear, about ten times the size of Ella.

That was definitely not on the list.

Ella squealed and went running for it, getting lost in the huge fluffy plush animal.

CULLEN

"Where do you want everything, ma'am?" he asked me, stepping into the foyer as I rescued Ella from the bear's embrace.

"Oh. You can just put it right here," I said. "I'll sort it out later."

And then I watched as he and another man made several trips, bringing in bags and boxes, filling his enormous foyer. I peeked into some of the bags and saw a wealth of baby paraphernalia. The baby proofing security stuff was there, as well . . . did he really buy a breast pump? What was he expecting I was going to do with that? I stopped breastfeeding over a year ago.

After about the tenth trip, I started to worry there wouldn't be enough space. "Just a couple more things, ma'am," the driver said, because I must've looked concerned.

The last thing they brought in was a brand-new toddler bed and mattress. And sheets with little pink elephants all over them.

Cullen must have had a saleslady helping him. I couldn't see him doing all of this himself.

About fifteen minutes later, he pulled up on his motorcycle as Ella and I were going through everything. The foyer looked a little like a Kids 'R Us.

"Did I do okay?" he asked, pulling off his helmet and scratching the back of his neck as he surveyed the disorder in the foyer.

I nodded, speechless, as I weaved my way around the piles of toys and clothes. I kissed him so hard, it struck him by surprise. When he broke the kiss, he grinned down at me.

"Guess that's a yes?"

I nodded, still unable to get the words out. I felt tears pinching the corners of my eyes.

Because the list of things he'd defend with no regard to his safety?

Right then, I knew Ella had made the cut.

Chapter Thirteen

Cullen

I looked around the fucking hellhole that had become my house and smiled.

My father, the old bastard, had moved in here when I was six or seven. The only toys he kept for me was a collection of Matchbox cars in a shoebox in the foyer closet, because he didn't want any of my shit fucking up his sweet bachelor pad. He always had the doors to the house open to anyone looking for a party. The liquor was always flowing, with endless lines of coke spread out on the dining room table.

But one thing he didn't want?

Kid stuff.

I finished putting together the toddler bed and arranged it by the window in the room we'd picked out for Ella, down the hall from my bedroom. "This good?" I asked Grace as I gave it a little shake for good measure to make sure it was sturdy.

She nodded. "Perfect. Thanks."

She was sitting on the floor, still wearing my t-shirt and a pair of short-shorts, going through all the stuff for Ella. Her hair was loose and messy and I was hoping it was naptime soon, because that meant I could get Grace into bed with me. She pulled out the sheets and started to make the bed.

Ella was playing with the blocks I'd gotten her, looking pretty damn happy. I had no fucking clue what a baby girl would play with, but the saleslady at the department store had been a big help. I told her to just fill up my cart with some of everything a new parent would need for their kid. And she did.

"Some of this we can return," Grace said, searching through the pile. "She's really too big for an exersaucer."

I looked at it. The picture on the side of the box showed a baby that I guessed was younger than Ella. "I have no fucking idea what that thing does."

CULLEN

"But it's nice," she added. "Thank you. I never had a baby shower for Ella. This kind of feels like that."

"Well, fuck," I said. "You should've had one."

"And invited who?" she asked, putting her hands on her hips and staring at me like I didn't have a clue about baby showers. Which I didn't.

"If you'd been with me, we could've invited a bunch of people."

"Yeah. I would just love to see all the Cobras at a freaking baby shower," she said with a grin. "We could've had finger sandwiches and played Guess the Baby's Birthdate. Isn't that what you normally do at church?"

I smirked. "Pretty much."

Just then, Ella collapsed against the giant bear she was wrestling with and yawned.

"Don't that mean she's tired?" I asked, lifting her up and setting the bear against the bed.

Grace gave me a suspicious look and shrugged. "Well, I don't know, what time is it?"

I checked my phone. "Three."

She contemplated this. "I usually put her down around four."

"Will the world end if you put her down early?" I cornered her against the wall, my hands on her bare arms, moving down and trying to cup her tits. No bra. Hell yes. I licked her earlobe. She pushed me away so fast I thought something was wrong. "What? I want to nail her mother."

She gave me the eye. "Not in front of Ella."

"Of course. But . . ." I looked over my shoulder at the kid, who was too busy babbling to the bear, trying to get it to talk to her. "I think we're good."

She stepped to the side. "She could turn around and see us in a heartbeat. My mother always had men all over her. I'm not doing that to Ella, understand?"

CULLEN

Letting out a breath, I pushed off the wall, just as my phone started to ring. I checked the screen. It was Hart. The king of bad timing.

I kissed Grace's temple and held up a finger. Stepping out of the room, I answered. "This better be good."

"When are you going to realize, man, it's always good when you're talking to me?" he said, pissing me off. Hart could really sling the bullshit. "You get in touch with the Fury yet?"

"For . . ." Shit. I'd been planning to get in touch with Slade and I hadn't. "Not yet. Wrapped up in things. I'll get to it tonight."

"Cool, man."

"That what you called me for? To be my warden?" I asked, peeking into the room. Grace was babbling baby talk to the kid, trying to get her to settle into her new bed. Fuck, yes. I'd obey the rules around Ella, but I couldn't wait to get Grace into my bedroom.

175

"No. Actually, I'm at the clubhouse. And there's a package over here for you, man," he said. "Says on it that it's urgent and needs to be opened right away."

"Who from?"

"Doesn't say."

Great. "I'll be over there after a while." I hadn't been planning on going anywhere tonight, but if it was Cobras business, it couldn't wait. Fuck. I knew Grace would give me shit about it.

"Good. Because you know, Dash and Jet were getting riled. You know. Wondering what the fuck is going down because you've been mum lately. Anything wrong?"

Of course they were. I was supposed to be setting up that meeting with Slade and all I've been doing is playing house here. I needed to focus. This wasn't how a president of a club behaved.

And if I let it go too long, the guys would try to take matters into their own hands. Especially Dash and

Jet, hotheads that they were. They'd fuck everything up.

"Nothing's wrong," I ground out.

"Any truth to the rumor going around that you got a kid?"

Fuck. I didn't want to get into this. I leaned into the phone and murmured, so Grace wouldn't hear, "A girl I used to know and her kid are staying with me, that's all. She was in trouble."

"All right, man. Don't get all fucked up about it."

I wasn't fucked up about it. Was I? Shit, my voice might have risen a notch. "Okay man, see you later."

I ended the call. I had to play this cooler than I was playing it. The last thing I needed was the Cobras wondering if I'd gone MIA on them. A president didn't do that. I could balance these things. I knew I could. I just needed Grace to understand that I had other things to deal with. Delicately, this time.

I went into the room as Grace was telling Ella a bedtime story, her eyes drooping closed. When she saw me her eyes popped opened and she smiled around her thumb. "New bed," she said.

Grace gave her a little hug. "I think she likes her new digs."

"Nice. Hey," I said. "Sorry but I've got to go. Cobras business."

She kissed Ella and stood up, following me out into the hallway. "Okay," she said, her voice breezy, but I knew better than that.

I got the feeling if I hadn't just bought out all of Target's baby department, I would've been in some serious shit.

I groaned as I wrapped my arms around her. Shit, she made it almost impossible to leave. She reached up and kissed me, long and slow. "You'll be home at a reasonable hour?"

"Girl, you and I both know that your reason and my reason ain't the same thing," I said with a grin. "But I'll be an hour or so, tops."

CULLEN

She gave me a doubtful look. "Cobras business? That means two."

"I'll bring home dinner. Okay?"

She nodded, satisfied. "Good. Don't make me miss you."

EVIE MONROE

CULLEN

Chapter Fourteen

Grace

Cullen wasn't the most punctual person on earth. Oh, he'd make sure church with the Cobras started at eight sharp. But when it came to how long he'd be gone when he said he was going out, I knew better than to take his word as gospel. I knew better than to make dinner plans or hang around waiting for him.

He was never on time when it came to me.

So when he said that he'd bring dinner home, I figured we'd probably end up eating at his dinnertime, which was ten at night. Having a baby that woke me up at daybreak, ten had quickly become my bedtime.

But as Ella napped, I decided to keep myself busy. There was a lot of work to be done, cleaning and baby-proofing the house. I got back to work, tossing all of the liquor bottles into the trash. Then I cleaned the kitchen, did some laundry, and baby-proofed most of the rooms that I thought Ella was likely to explore.

When I was done, I felt a little better about having Ella in the house. The place was more like a home and a bit less like a bachelor pad.

I looked at the clock and realized it was after five. He'd been gone almost two hours already.

Sighing, I climbed the stairs. I needed to get Ella up or else she wouldn't sleep at night. When I got her up, I decided to feed her dinner in the brand new high chair that Cullen had bought for her. I fixed a chicken breast and vegetables and when she started chomping on it, my stomach started to grumble.

When my stomach grumbled for mashed carrots and peas and bland chicken, I knew I had a problem. I was starving.

Ella was wide awake, so I read a book to her but mostly I chased her from room to room. Where was Cullen? Not only was I starving, but my little darling was wearing me out. It was past six, almost six-thirty.

CULLEN

Cullen had made it clear he didn't want me to leave. He'd armed the alarm when he left and told me to stay put. But that was fine as long as he would be holding up his end of the bargain and *coming home when he Goddamn said he would.*

Which he wouldn't.

Ella had been cooped up in the house all. She needed to get out and get some fresh air. Hell, I needed to get out. Maybe I'd take Ella to the beach. And stop by the clubhouse and tell him to hurry his ass up.

That was actually a good idea. For so long, Cullen had always acted like it was either the Cobras or me. Like he couldn't have both; he could only choose one or the other. I was sure the other Cobras had probably heard stories about me being an old ball and chain. He'd probably told them that I couldn't deal with him being a Cobra and I'd constantly nagged him to quit it. If I showed up and was supportive, maybe he wouldn't see the Cobras and me as two opposing sides. Maybe he wouldn't feel the need to put me second. Maybe he'd realize we could definitely work this out.

A plan filled my mind as I finished scraping up the last of the carrots from the container. Yes, he'd said that church was sacred. Members only. What happened at church, stayed at church. But Cullen was president and used to bending the rules. Plus, if I showed up in my little black number, he'd never be able to hold a grudge.

I wiped Ella's mouth with a bib. "Want to see where daddy works?" I asked her.

She nodded excitedly and clapped her hands.

All right. I'd gone through a bunch of papers during the clean-up spree and located an address on the bay for a warehouse he was renting. I figured that had to be the clubhouse. I lifted the receiver on his phone and called for a cab.

Then I went upstairs, dressed myself in my slinkiest black dress, and put Ella in her cutest red romper. "Two hot mamas, out on the town, right girl?" I said as I propped her up on the sink and wet her curls to bounce them back into ringlets.

CULLEN

"Mama," she said, pointing at my reflection.

"Yes, baby. Let's go see daddy. He's got a date with us."

When I finished brushing my hair and applying lip gloss, I looked out the window and saw the cab there. Cullen had a stack of cash in his armoire and had told me to help myself. So I lifted some twenties from the stack and stuffed them into my purse.

Then I disarmed the alarm to step outside and hurried to the cab with Ella in my arms.

EVIE MONROE

Chapter Fifteen

Cullen

On the way to the clubhouse, I stopped in at The Wall, just to have a beer and gauge what the rumor mill was spurting out. Zain was there, had just gotten back from a shift at the garage, and he and I ended up talking for a while, since he was the one with the inside scoop on what the Fury was up to.

"Still quiet," he said to me with a shrug, spinning bottle caps on the bar. "Never heard them so quiet before. If I didn't know better, I'd think they dropped off the face of the earth."

"Means trouble, you think?"

Vera, a tight piece of ass who was the bartender at The Wall most nights and Zain's main action—mostly because she gave us free drinks—refilled our shot glasses with tequila without us asking. Zain winked at her and said, "Nah. You never know with Slade. I mean, Blaze was a loose cannon, but Slade's even more fucked in the head. He alternates between touched and just good old, straight-up batshit."

"Yeah?" I tossed back the shot and signaled to Vera for another one. And this was the guy I was going to be having a nice, friendly conversation with? Couldn't wait.

"Hey. Thought you were going to meet with him. Did you ever get in touch with him?"

"Yeah. For the last time. I'm gonna. Gonna give him a call tonight and set it up." I punched him. "Geez, fucking Christ, you guys nag worse than a bunch of bitches on the rag."

He grinned at me and popped a handful of peanuts into his mouth. "Speaking of bitches. I hear you have one at home at the famous McKnight bachelor pad. Isn't that against your rules?"

Holy hell, news about me did not miss anyone. I thought of Grace, all hot and gorgeous in my bed, the way her skin felt under my touch, the way she looked, curled up in my sheets. A pretty little dream, one I couldn't wait to wake up to. "Yeah. An ex. Just visiting."

"Gotcha." He raised an eyebrow and continued feeding himself peanuts. I got the feeling he didn't believe me. *Change the subject, Cullen.*

"So, back to Slade. You think he'll shut me down? You think he won't want to talk it out?"

Zain slumped over the bar. "See, that's the thing with Slade. You just can't fucking read him. He likes to be the mystery man. Leaves you guessing."

The prospects for our phone call were looking bleaker by the moment. "Yeah? So when you were on that side . . .what were your dealings with him?"

"Didn't have much interaction with him at all. You know, never around much but when he was around he was too important to associate with any of us new or potential Fury. Just heard from everyone he was a bad bitch, and to stay away. You didn't want to piss in his Cheerios, that's for sure."

I scrubbed a hand over my face. "Sounds great."

"Yeah. Like there was this one time. He came in, all quiet, like it was just another day. Then he grabbed a pool cue and fucked up another Fury. I mean, left him bleeding on the fucking floor in pieces. Punctured his lung, broke nearly all his ribs, just went off on him for like twenty minutes straight, and no one dared stop him. Guy nearly died." He shook his head and exhaled. "Come to find out Slade's girl was fucking around with him, and he'd done worse to her, at home. Practically killed her."

Reasonable fucker. I sucked in a breath. Yeah. This little talk was not going to go over well. But I still had to try. I'd promised Hart and Zain I would give them the chance, and I still wasn't convinced we needed to launch into an all-out war.

I checked my phone and slipped off the stool. Shit, I was going to be a lot later than I told Grace. I'd said only an hour, but I'd spent more than an hour shooting the shit with Zain.

She knew me. She knew I was never on time for anything.

CULLEN

Though I had to be out of my mind. I had her waiting at home for me. Sexy, fucking beautiful, everything I could possibly want. In my bed. I didn't know how I managed to stay away.

"Going to the clubhouse now," I told Zain, pulling out my wallet and dropping a couple twenties on the bar. "Thought I'd see what was going on and make the call from there. You coming?"

He grabbed his helmet. "Yeah."

The two of us went outside, got on our bikes, and set out toward the pier. When we got to the warehouse, I saw Hart's bike there, as well as a few bikes of some of the other guys. As I climbed off my bike, there was a stiff wind coming off the ocean, and what looked like a storm blowing in. Just as we were opening the door to the clubhouse, lightning lit up the sky.

The clubhouse was, as usual, hazy with cigarette smoke. Led Zeppelin wafted from the speakers, almost drowning out the sound of pool balls clacking together.

"Hey!" Hart called to me, looking up from his game of pool as I fist-bumped the other guys inside. I'd been here only a few days before, but it felt like I'd been gone forever. Before Grace, I used to come to the clubhouse every day. This place was probably more my home than the mansion ever was.

Hart pointed a finger toward the kitchen. I peeked into the small room and noted the package he'd mentioned on the phone, which he'd left on the counter for me. It was about the size of a helmet and wrapped in craft paper. Probably some parts I'd ordered for the cars. I had other business to deal with first and lit up a cigarette.

We had a landline attached to a pole in the kitchen area and I headed for it to make my call. Zain and Hart came up close, wanting to hear the conversation. Hart gave me a piece of paper, with the number written on it. I dialed, dragging on my smoke as I waited for someone to pick up.

On the fourth ring, when I thought it was going to voicemail, someone said, "Talk to me."

CULLEN

I squeezed my opposite ear closed so I wouldn't hear Robert Plant's screeching "Whole Lotta Love." I shot Zain a look and he turned down the music. I traded a glance with Hart as I said, "Hey. This Slade?"

"Yep. Who am I talking to?" His voice was smooth. Deep. In control.

"Cullen."

"Cullen." He said it like one would say *Herpes*. "I've heard about you. Bastard who killed Blaze and four of my men. Am I right?"

"You got your information wrong, Slade," I said, straddling a stool in front of a 70's orange laminate kitchen counter and pulling an ashtray over. "Blaze wasn't playing by the rules. Kidnapping an innocent girl? We couldn't let that slide. You gotta know that."

He snorted. "I'll give you that. He didn't get much in the brains department, ol' Blaze. I was just listening to a little bit of The Fritz on the radio. Your daddy sure could *play*, man. I'm a guitar man myself. You got any of that talent?"

"No," I muttered. My father had talent, but I'd known from a young age I wanted to be nothing like Brent McKnight. Never even picked up a guitar. "Wasn't that lucky."

"Ah, too bad. So what is the leader of the goddamn Steel Cobras doing, calling me on this fine night?" he said. It sounded like he was chewing on something.

Cocky asshole. I could just see him, sitting on his fucking throne.

I took another drag, choosing my words carefully, thinking of all the intel Zain had given me on this crazy bitch. "I think now's a good time for the two of our clubs to see if we can't find some common ground. There's plenty of Aveline Bay for all of us, and I want you and I to hash it out. See what we can do."

There was silence. Then, he laughed, long and hard. "You mean, peace and harmony, sixties hippie shit?"

"Yeah."

CULLEN

He said, smoothly, "I like the way you think, man. You know. We lost some men last month with the business that went on, including Blaze. I was just telling the guys it was needless shit. It didn't have to happen."

He sounded reasonable. I felt good about this. "Yeah, man. So name the time and place. I'll be there."

Suddenly, thunder rumbled overhead, the walls of the warehouse shaking. "Just us two?"

"Yeah. No need to involve anyone else. Let's just sit down and have a few beers."

"All right. Then let's do Rocky's." Rocky's was a bar downtown, on neutral turf. "Say, tomorrow at eight?"

"Sounds good."

"I'll be there, Cullen my man. We lost five men, so I can't promise you this'll fix things. But, I can promise you the Fury ain't going anywhere."

"Understood." I cut the call and looked at the guys. They all had surprised looks on their faces, like they'd expected the call would erupt in a shouting match. I was pretty surprised myself. Hadn't thought it'd go that smoothly. I thought I'd get a lot more shit than I had. Especially since we'd killed five of their guys.

"We got a meeting," I said, stubbing out the end of the cigarette. "Tomorrow at eight. Rocky's."

Zain punched his palm. "Shit. I didn't think he'd bite, truly. Can I go with?"

I snorted at him. Of all the Cobras, they hated Zain most of all, since he was once almost one of them. "I'm going alone."

"You think that's smart?" Hart asked, running a hand through his ruddy hair.

"It's fine. That's what we agreed on. I ain't worried."

Hart let out a short laugh. "Since when do the Fury ever play by the rules? Honor doesn't mean nothing to them."

CULLEN

I threw up my hands. He was right. But just because it didn't mean anything to them, it didn't mean I was just going to let the Cobras code go. "I'm not going to worry about that until there's something to worry about. Right now, we're just two guys, going out for beers. That's it."

Hart shot me a doubtful look and crossed his thick, tattooed arms. Fine. I'd let him and the others wait in a parking lot nearby, if it'd make them feel better.

Then I looked at my phone. Seven o'clock. Hell, I'd now been gone for over four hours. I wasn't scared of this Slade asshole who'd nearly impaled a guy on a pool cue because I'd seen what a livid Grace could do, and it wasn't pretty.

Shit shit shit. I'd go pick her up a really nice dinner. Then I'd take her into bed and by the end of the night she'd have screamed my name so much that she'd have forgotten I was late. "I got to go, guys," I announced to them, pocketing my phone. "I got plans."

I grabbed my helmet and made toward the door, for the first time hearing what sounded like armies marching across the corrugated metal roof. Fuck, the rain was coming down. Out the window, all I could see was a wall of gray.

"Wow, man," Hart breathed, peering out the window. "Look at it coming down. Never seen it rain this hard. You going out in that?"

I couldn't remember the last time it'd rained. The roads would be slick as hell, not to mention I probably wouldn't be able to see shit. Yeah, I'd wait for the rain to slow. Grace would understand. She'd bitch, but eventually, she'd understand.

Then I looked over on the counter and saw the package.

Setting down my helmet, I walked toward the counter and picked it up. Tossed it in my hands. It was surprisingly heavy. Shook it a little. Something inside shifted.

CULLEN

Our parts didn't come in like this. They were clearly marked by the vendor. That set off alarm bells in my head. But like I said, I wasn't going to worry until there was something to worry about.

I studied the name on it. The name and mailing address had been hand-written in block lettering. No return address. No shipping information. So it hadn't come from the post, or UPS, or FedEx. "Who dropped this off?" I asked Hart.

He shrugged. "It was at the door when I got here."

Wiping at my eye, I went to get a knife to rip it open when I suddenly heard something. Beeping. Like a timer. Beep. Beep. Beep.

Shit.

I brought the package to my ear.

The rhythmic sound was definitely coming from inside.

And I doubted someone had sent me a timer as a gift.

"Fuck," I breathed, sliding the package onto the table and dropping the knife. I backed toward the door. "Everyone out! It's a fucking bomb!"

They all looked up at once, and then they began to stampede toward the door. I threw it open, into a wall of rain, just as another jagged slice of lightning lit up the sky and thunder began to rumble.

A bomb. A fucking bomb. No wonder that asshole Slade was so agreeable. And I was playing right into his hands.

I motioned for them all to hurry, shouting at them to get their asses moving, when I looked through the steady downpour to the parking lot and saw a taxi slowing to a stop at the end of the docks.

Rain soaked my face, matting my hair against my eyes as I stood in the open door and watched Grace slip out of the taxi, holding Ella in one arm, a pink jacket tenting her head.

Grace. Fuck. What the fuck was she doing here?

CULLEN

She knew not to come to church. I'd told her to stay away.

But since when did Grace ever do a fucking thing I told her to?

My chest squeezed. I gritted my teeth as she bumped the door closed with her hip and started to run my way.

I waved at her, but she had the jacket over her face, shielding me from her view. I shouted as loud as I could, but the rain raged around us, drowning out my voice.

She kept coming.

Fear knotted in my chest. Too close. This was bad.

I let go of the door and broke into a run, waving both arms at her and shouting my fucking head off.

EVIE MONROE

Chapter Sixteen

Grace

We didn't get much rain in Aveline Bay.

But as I stepped out to the cab and placed Ella in the back seat, I could smell it coming, feel it in the wind. I looked up and saw dark, menacing clouds approaching from the ocean, just as thunder started to rumble in the distance.

Barry was out in front, holding a stack of mail in her hands. "Looks like we're going to get a whopper!" she called to me, pointing to the sky. "Stay dry and safe!"

I waved to her. "I will! Thanks!"

I slid into the car and said to the driver, a middle-aged bald man with dark skin, "Thanks for getting here so quickly," and closed the door behind me.

"Hey, sweetie," he said to me, smiling at Ella. "Looks like we're about to get a little rain. Let's see if we can't get you where you want to go before it starts to pour."

"That would be great." I looked over at Ella as the driver pulled out of Cullen's long drive, thinking a walk by the beach probably wasn't the smartest idea ever, considering. I'd written the address of the clubhouse on my palm. "Can you take me to 121 Ocean Avenue instead?"

He nodded, raising an eyebrow. "That's on the pier. Bunch of warehouses there. Rough area. What you and your sweet baby want with going all the way out there?"

I smiled. "Just meeting someone."

He shrugged and didn't ask any more questions. Even put on a CD with songs like "Wheels on the Bus" and "Where is Thumbkin?" much to Ella's glee and she sat on my lap and sang along. He was one of those cab drivers who rambled on, so by the time we got downtown, I'd found out he had four grandchildren of his own and had lived in the Bay all his life, just like me. He asked me all about Ella. Ella, fed and rested,

CULLEN

wrapped her chubby arms around me and grinned happily.

We drove past downtown Aveline Bay, past the homeless shelter, past the Best Western, and then he hung a left and steered us down the long pier, past dozens of vast buildings surrounded by shipping containers and machinery. And yes, a few tough-looking guys, milling about, but that didn't faze me. Cullen was the king of tough guys. Around him, I wouldn't have to worry.

I held Ella up so she could look out the window, just as the first raindrops pinged against the glass, thinking about the one time Cullen and I had gone out to The Wall, the Cobras' favorite watering hole. I'd met some of the Cobras for the first time; Hart and Nix and Drake . . . each one bigger and tougher and hotter than the next. But none could hold a candle to Cullen, and they all respected Cullen something fierce.

It was easy to see why they'd choose him to be their president.

That night, I'd had a little too much to drink and grabbed a shot of tequila off the bar, downing it, when a huge tough guy, with arms the size of tree trunks, spun on the bar. "Hey, that was my drink, bitch!"

I'd started to apologize when Cullen nudged me behind him and confrontationally pushed his chest out. "Who the fuck are you calling a bitch, motherfucker?"

Cullen didn't give a shit that the guy had five inches on him. He shoved him square in the chest, and the man stumbled back against his stool, stunned.

Cullen got right in his face. "Apologize to her. It's a fucking honor to buy her a drink, asshole. Now thank her for letting you," he growled, pulling him up by the shirt and forcing him to look at me.

The guy blinked, confused. He looked more at the ground than at me, face reddening. "Hey, um, thanks for letting me buy you a drink . . ."

"See? That wasn't so hard." Cullen slammed a bill onto the counter. "But that one was actually on me."

CULLEN

Then he patted the guy's cheek, took me by the elbow, and led me out of the bar. I'd only gone to the bar with him once, but from the way the men were grinning at him and the women's tongues were wagging as their eyes followed him out of the place, this was a regular occurrence.

I'd never been so proud to be with him then at that moment. Or turned on. The sex we'd had that night? Fan-fucking-tastic.

I blinked out of the memory when the sky opened, like God just dumped a massive bucket of water over all of Aveline Bay.

"Wow." The driver slowed and turned his windshield wipers way up. "Sorry, dear. Looks like you're going to be getting a little wet."

His headlights cut through the rain, but steam was rising from the overheated streets, cutting visibility way down. I could barely see a thing. He inched along as lightning lit up the sky around us. "That's okay. Geez. It's really coming down, isn't it?"

"Yeah, boy." He tightened his hands on the steering wheel. "Tell you what. We get to your address and you stay in here as long as you like. I won't leave the meter running."

I smiled gratefully at him. "Thank you. But your time is just as valuable as mine. I'm sure you have other places to be. And I'll only be a few minutes. I'll want you to stay, anyway, because I think I'll need a ride back."

I looked at what I'd brought with me and gauged the situation. I had a new diaper bag that Cullen had bought, and it didn't have much in it but diapers. No raincoats. No umbrella. I'd packed Ella's pink changing pad. Maybe that could serve as a little something to keep us from getting drenched? I pulled it out and unrolled it. It was pretty big. It was worth a shot.

I peered through the gray rain as we continued down to the harbor until I saw about ten motorcycles, all lined up against the side of a one-story white building. There was a silhouette of what might have been an old company sign on the wall, but right now

CULLEN

the only words I could make out was the address. 121 Ocean Avenue.

The door opened and I saw someone with a leather motorcycle jacket and helmet under his arm jogging out. Definitely the right place.

I scooped Ella into my arms and held the changing pad over our heads. "Thank you!" I said, jumping out into an ankle-deep puddle in the driving rain and wishing I hadn't worn such a tight, short dress.

It quickly became clear the pad wasn't doing shit. The rain was whipping in sideways, pelting us both, loud as a drumbeat in my ears. Ella squealed, delighted by the feeling.

Head down, I hugged Ella close to me and raced to the entrance, vaguely aware that the door was open for me. Maybe Cullen saw me and was coming out to help.

When I got closer, though, I heard noise. Shouts. I looked up, blinking away raindrops to see men out there. The Cobras. They were running out. Where were they going?

I slowed when I saw Cullen, standing at the door of the warehouse, his mouth opened in a scream.

What the hell was going on?

When I slowed to a stop and strained to hear, I heard him shout two things: *Get* and *back*.

He started to race for me. I froze. "What?" I called. Ella looked up at me, her chubby, rain-spattered face growing frightened. Dropping the changing pad, I cupped her head and rested her against my chest. "What's going on?"

I'd never seen his face as urgent and downright determined as it had been right then. He reached for me, spun me around, and yelled, "Run! Get out of here!"

We broke into a run, and suddenly, the world around us rippled and exploded. For a moment, everything went black, Ella screamed, there was a deafening blast, and then, the only thing I could hear

CULLEN

was my own heartbeat. The ground pushed up and we were flung forward. A scream trapped itself in my throat as we were thrown to the ground. I braced Ella against me to avoid the impact but something—or someone—was bracing me.

We hit the pavement with a thud. The only thing I sensed was the warmth of his body, his strong arms, cocooning us, making sure that he'd never let anything—or anyone—hurt us.

EVIE MONROE

Chapter Seventeen

Cullen

Pain seared up my neck. On the ground, I looked over my shoulder to see if we were in the clear. The warehouse was demolished. Black smoke poured into the air and flames licked at the walls and hunks of twisted metal. Ash and debris floated down on us, along with the steady, driving rain. In the distance, my guys were running through the curtains of smoke, some shouting, others with their mouths open.

But I couldn't hear them. Couldn't hear the roar of the fire. All I could hear was the echo of my heart in my head. I pressed a hand to my ear. It came back wet and sticky with my blood.

I turned to Grace, who was huddled in a ball on the ground, still clutching Ella. Ella's face was contorted in a sob I couldn't hear. Grace's chest heaved.

EVIE MONROE

I reached out and grabbed her face in my hands, steadying her. "You okay?" I asked, looking her over. She had a bleeding scratch on her cheek, mixing with raindrops. I yanked off my *kutte* and then my shirt to stop the bleeding, but it wasn't very clean. It was covered in blood, but I brought it to her cheek.

We were soaked to the skin now. Her body trembled. She grabbed Ella, doing the same inspection I'd done to Grace. Her mouth moved in a frantic twist as she examined the little girl, but I couldn't understand her. I turned to Ella, who was still sobbing, red-faced, and saw what Grace saw: Ella's face was bloody.

I looked closer, for the source. "It's not her." I said, sounding like I was talking in slow motion. "It's your blood. Mine."

She grabbed Ella to her chest and heaved a sigh of relief.

I pounded on the side of my head, willing my hearing back, and it worked some, because I heard her voice, but far away. "You. You're bleeding, Cullen." She reached for me and I followed her line of sight, feeling my neck. Warm, wet blood was pouring down my back. I lifted my hand and found the source of the bleeding, a cut on the back of my head.

"I'm okay," I said.

Behind me, I heard the shouts of people, and in the distance, sirens. The rain pounded harder all around us.

I motioned to a bus shelter with a bench at the side of the pier. I lifted Grace to her feet and dragged her and Ella over there. I wiped the gravel from her knees and shins as she perched at the edge of the bench. "Stay here, okay? I'll be back."

She hugged Ella and nodded absently, the two of them wet and shivering. Thunder boomed overhead, and she shook.

I took her face in my hand and made her look at me. "Hey. It's going to be okay. You good?"

She blinked with recognition and nodded again, this time, more with it.

As fast as the rain had come on, now it was starting to let up. I ran down to where Hart was standing, talking with some of the other guys. Everyone looked fine, just soaked. "Everyone get out?"

He nodded. "Shit, that was a close one," he breathed out, surveying the damage. "Ripped a fucking hole in our operations, though. What the fuck?"

Zain jogged up a second later, nursing a bleeding gash that had cemented his eye shut. Out of breath, he doubled over with his hands on his knees. Then he said the word that all of us were thinking. "Fury."

Yeah. I nodded. Shit. No wonder he'd been so nice and accommodating on the phone. I'd played right into it like a fucking moron. Slade wouldn't let us off that easy without some revenge, no matter what he said. Zain had even said that dude could be unpredictable and had a fucking sadistic streak.

I looked back toward the bench, where Ella and Grace were huddled together.

He'd gotten close. Too close. Any closer, and . . .

CULLEN

"So what do we do?" Hart asked.

Zain punched his fist. "We go after them and blow a fucking hole in their heads."

I held up my hands. The first responders had barely arrived and they were talking about getting revenge? No. I didn't even know if everyone was okay yet.

We had to think this through. It was not having a chance to think this through that had gotten us into the situation where we'd had to kill some of Fury's men. We were on a path that would only mean a lot more casualties, and I wasn't about to lose any men. "Relax. For now. We have to be smart about this. Let's wait for the dust to settle."

The fire trucks screamed in, sirens blaring, and Jet and Drake came in, right behind, on their cycles. I braced myself as they got off their bikes, knowing exactly where those two assholes stood. "Jesus," Jet said, scrubbing his hands through his hair. He looked at me. "*Now* are we going to do something?"

EVIE MONROE

I didn't look at him. That was Jet, just willing to jump in without knowing the whole story. He didn't even know what had happened. Zain cupped his hands around his mouth and lit a cigarette, then offered one to me, which I took. "Cool it," I muttered to Jet, striding over to the fire chief as his men fought to put out the blaze.

"It was a bomb," I called over to him, lighting the cigarette. "We all got out."

The fire chief regarded me like most of the city did, with annoyed indifference. We'd have to start paying these guys more money. "Where'd this bomb come from?" he asked.

"It was a package, delivered to us," I said as an ambulance pulled up behind us. When the EMTs got out, two guys looked at my head, which was bleeding its way down my back. I waved them away and motioned to Grace and Ella. "Forget me. See to them."

"Don't be a hard ass. That needs stitches," Drake said, trying to touch it.

CULLEN

I grunted and wiped the blood away. "Later."

The EMT glanced at the wound and said, "He's right. And we have to check for a concussion."

Of course Drake was right, but I wasn't going to the hospital right now and leaving my club. I had other things on my mind. As far as I was concerned, my brains weren't leaking from my head, so no problem. "Like I said, *later*," I muttered, taking a drag of the cigarette to calm my nerves as I strode toward the wreckage. Under a pile of blown-up corrugated metal, I saw the remains of a motorcycle. "What did we lose?"

"Fuck!" Hart groaned. "My fucking bike is under there. My dad gave me that bike."

I nodded. Hart loved that piece of shit, because his dad had been his hero. "I'll get you another one. What else?"

"How about our dignity?" Jet said. He and Drake were the only ones of us who didn't look like we'd just gone to hell and back. We were covered head to toe in black, and Jet looked even more like a lily-white pretty boy than usual. He hadn't lost a thing.

I gave him a look and he backed down. He was lucky he was Nix's brother or I would've given him a hell of a lot worse.

"Look, guys. I know we're all riled right now. But let's take a breath, can we?" I checked my phone. It was just after seven. I looked at Hart. "Church. Ten."

Jet snorted. "Where?"

This place was a circus right now with the fire trucks, ambulances, curious onlookers, and now a news helicopter was circling overhead. Couldn't very well discuss this in the open. I sure as hell wasn't going to bring them to my house. Not with Grace and Ella there. "The garage."

They all nodded.

I tossed the cigarette stub on the ground and went back to Grace and Ella, who were just finishing up with the EMT. Grace had a band-aid on her cheek, now. She handed me my shirt, and I shrugged it on. I pointed to the cab she'd come in on. The driver was still there, filming everything on his cell phone. "You should go back to the house."

She nodded and pointed at my head. "But what about you? You need to get to the—"

"Stop. I'll live. I'll have Drake patch it up later."

"But . . .?"

"Relax. Drake's got this. He was a doc in another life."

She eyed me doubtfully and her brows knitted together. "So what was it? Hell's Fury, again? Why are they doing this to you? Shooting your house and then bombing your meeting place? Do they want you dead?"

I shook my head. "Shut up. I don't know. Don't even know if it was them. That's what we're going to figure out." I looked back at the guys, who I could tell were getting more riled by the minute. They all needed me to deliver a dose of calm-the-fuck-down. "But, I need you out of here. Now."

She looked down that Ella, who was dozing off, her head falling against Grace's chest. Finally, she nodded, and I walked her over to the cab and helped her inside. I closed the door and banged on the roof of the car. As it took off, I turned to see Zain jogging toward me.

I knew what he was going to say before he said it. "That the ex who's staying at your house? What the fuck was she here for?"

I motioned to him to give me another cigarette and lit it. I only smoked like a chimney during shit like this. "No clue."

"That your kid?"

I rubbed at my jaw, ignoring the question. Zain might've been our newest member, but he knew enough that when I didn't answer, it wasn't that I didn't hear him. It meant to back the fuck off.

I went back toward the smoldering club house and watched the firefighters going back and forth from the building. The flames were almost out. I joined the guys and said, "Look. All of you. We still don't know if this came from Slade."

"Who else could it have come from?" Hart asked.

"Yeah, it's a good chance. But we made a lot of enemies that night. There's no saying that the bomb wasn't just one of the members, trying to get their own revenge. And it's not like Hell's Fury are the only people who've ever been after us. Right?"

Zain didn't agree with me on this. I could see it in his eyes. "But this is the mark of someone straight-up batshit. Slade."

Jet nodded. Goddammit, the guy was always doing shit to undermine me. He was such a little pisser that I think if authority told him the sky was blue he'd argue just to have something to argue about.

Just then, Nix pulled up on his bike. "Holy shit," he said, ripping off his helmet. "Fury?"

I took a slow drag of my cigarette. "That's what we're trying to figure out. I'm not jumping to conclusions."

He frowned as his eyes swept over my head. "Anyone hurt?"

"Not bad."

"Jesus. You could see the smoke from the garage."

My phone buzzed in my pocket. I lifted it out, expecting it to be one of my guys, asking what the hell was going on. But it was an unknown number. I answered it. "Yeah?"

"Saw you on the news," a voice said, low and confident.

Slade.

My jaw tensed. I didn't have his number until Hart pulled it out, and I'd called him from the land line at the clubhouse. How had he gotten my cell number?

The answer was one I didn't want to think about: He was hunting us.

I turned away from the guys and put a finger to my other ear so I could hear over the sea wind.

CULLEN

"Is this your fucking work, Slade?" I growled into the phone.

The guys turned silent and began to crowd around me as he said, "You're looking good without your shirt. You been working out? But that cut on your head should probably be looked at."

"Don't fuck with me," I muttered.

"Aw. What happened to friendly beers at Rocky's?" He let out a low laugh. "That's one thing you need to understand, boy. We're. Not. Friends."

I sucked on my cigarette, not meeting the eyes of my guys, who were studying me with bloody murder on their faces. "I won't make that mistake again."

"That package was just a message. And the next time I see you, that little cut on your head'll be nothing compared to what we do to you. You got that?"

"Don't think we're going down without a fight," I said, squaring my shoulders, adrenaline coursing through my veins. He messed with the wrong mother fuckin' club. "You just declared yourself a war."

EVIE MONROE

CULLEN

Chapter Eighteen

Grace

The second I got into the taxi and it started to pull away, the kind old driver wiped his face with a handkerchief and began to chatter like there was no tomorrow.

"Damn, that was the craziest thing I ever saw! I thought for sure we were goners. What the . . . wow. If you'd gone in there only a second earlier . . ."

I let him go on and on, thinking about the roar of the bomb, the way it'd felt like someone had pulled the ground out from under me, the white-hot bolt of fear that had shot through me like a bullet before I hit the ground, the half-formed, frantic thoughts of protecting Ella that had blazed through my mind, blotting out everything else.

Cullen had to have had those thoughts, too. Of protecting us. I could still feel his strong arms around me as he wrapped us up tight, taking the brunt of the damage.

The way he'd looked at me, like I was something precious... no, like I was the most precious thing he'd ever had... would've taken my breath away if I wasn't already gasping from the force of the impact.

I knew he cared. He maybe even loved us.

But I also knew it wasn't enough.

Watching him talk to the Cobras, I could see how they needed him. I could see that they all respected him and fell in line to listen to him. He was good at what he did, and I understood why he felt the need to do it.

But his life as part of the Cobras wasn't what I'd thought. It was so much worse.

I could live with him being in a club. I could maybe even live with him thinking that those men were more important than Ella and me. I loved him enough that I probably could put up with that. But that was the least of it. Our house being shot at? Bombs going off?

CULLEN

Living in a war zone? Never knowing if he would come home to me alive?

No. I didn't know if I could live like that, much less put Ella in a war zone. And honestly, I didn't want to find out.

I'd always promised myself that I'd never let Ella see me cry, or yell, or do anything that could scare her. But I couldn't help it. She was nodding off against my shoulder, anyway. I drew her baby soft curls to my head and began to sob quietly.

"Hey," the kindly driver said to me as we drove away from the harbor. "It's all right. You're safe."

For now. But how much longer? I swiped at my eyes with the back of my hand. "I'm sorry. I'm just really shaken up."

"Yeah. It was something. Is he your boyfriend?" he asked.

I shook my head. "No. A . . . friend, I guess."

He nodded. "He's a tough motorcycle guy, huh? Looked a little like a thug. Not someone for a nice girl like you. Was the bomb meant for him and his crew?"

I shrugged, even though I knew the answer.

"He's up to no good, huh? I don't know. I know I'm not your dad, but my gut says to stay away from that kind of thing. Bad kid."

I pressed my lips together. Yeah. My gut was saying the same thing.

I still loved him. But I couldn't do this. I couldn't live like this.

I had to leave and take Ella far away from him, and I couldn't wait. If I did, Cullen would convince me to stay. I had absolutely no willpower where he was concerned. He probably wouldn't be home until much later, now that he had so much to take care of. If I was going to leave, I'd have to do it while he was away. The thought sent a pang of sadness and a surge of panic through me.

CULLEN

Just more moving, never setting down roots. The story of my life.

The rain had stopped by the time we got to the house. I pulled Ella's sleeping body to my chest, handing the rest of my money to the driver. Then I took a deep breath.

"Do you think you could wait here? And take me someplace else?"

"Of course. Where is this someplace else, dear?"

Someplace else. I hadn't even thought about where I could go. All my life, I'd never left the bay, and the thought of stepping outside the boundaries of the place I'd always lived filled me with dread. There was a whole wide world out there, which I knew nothing about. I didn't even know where to start.

But when he asked, it came to me right away. A place where I could easily disappear.

"Los Angeles," I said, fear skittering through my body.

EVIE MONROE

"Los Angeles?" He let out a whoop. "Girl, it's nearly eight-thirty. We won't get there until after midnight. You sure? That baby of yours sure looks sleepy."

I looked at her. Yes, I could stay for her, but that would only help her for the short term. I needed to leave for her future. "Yes. I'm sure."

I slipped out of the cab, slammed the door, and hurried toward the house, where I disarmed the security system and quickly slipped inside. I laid Ella down in her bed, went to the bathroom and looked at myself long and hard in the mirror.

My face was covered with dust and ash from the explosion, my eye make-up streaked down on my cheeks. I scrubbed my face in the sink, then slipped off the little black dress and put on a pair of cut-offs, a camisole, and flip-flops.

Then I found my suitcase and started to load it up with as much clothing as it would hold for Ella and me. When it was so stuffed I had to sit on it to close and zip it up, I opened Cullen's armoire and pulled out another thousand dollars. He'd mind that I was gone again, sure, but he wouldn't care about the money. Knowing him, he wouldn't even notice it was gone.

As I went through the house, I found myself weakening as I looked at all the unopened toys and kid things he'd bought. Just when this house was starting to look like a home. My eyes caught on the giant teddy bear that Ella had fallen in love with. We'd have to leave it all behind.

This was all so close to the dream. It even looked like the dream.

But it was all an illusion.

I finished packing the suitcase, then wheeled it outside. The cab driver put it in the trunk for me. Then I went back to get Ella. She was sound asleep in her toddler bed, with the soft elephant sheets and new pink blanket. She looked so cozy.

I stifled a sob as I lifted her out. It was getting late, and we had to make it to L.A.

EVIE MONROE

Chapter Nineteen

Cullen

"Jesus," I muttered, shouldering Drake in the ribs. "Take it easy."

I'd had Drake patch up countless injuries in the past, but I couldn't remember one hurting quite so much. I sat there, holding my hair out of the way, as he dug the needle into my scalp again. "What, you got ants in your pants? Stop jiggling around like that."

I let out a hard breath and checked my phone. It was after nine. The fire had burned out fast and the emergency vehicles had been on their way in within the hour. Most of the guys had gotten to Lucky Leaf early, since after the explosion, they were too wired to do anything else. There were rumors flying all over the place. I'd need to settle them down, and quick.

Lucky Leaf was Hart's father's place, and where most of the guys in the Cobras worked in some form or another. Hart had never been a mechanic but Nix, Jet, and Drake were. They'd gotten to know each other through the garage before they'd become officers in the club.

The garage was small, with no waiting room, just three bays, two of them occupied by cars up on lifts. We'd all crammed into the third bay for church, by the shithole business office. The place was choked with smoke, but I wasn't going to open a garage door and risk the chance of a Fury seeing us. With our clubhouse destroyed, there weren't too many other places to hold our meetings.

"Done?" I asked Drake as he stuck the needle into my skin once again.

He yanked on it, then leaned forward, biting the ends of the suture and freeing the needle. He ran a finger over it. "Aw, that looks pretty."

I shoved him away, messing a hand through my hair to get it to fall over the stitching. My hair was sticky with blood. I needed a shower almost as much as I needed a drink. I lit another cigarette as Drake sat

CULLEN

down next to Nix and Jet, then I boosted myself up onto the workbench. "Okay, guys. Let's get this party started."

The room silenced.

"First of all. Is everyone okay?"

There were nods, and Zain and Hart said yes. "What happened?" Nix asked.

"A package arrived at the clubhouse . . ." I looked at Hart. "When?"

Hart shrugged. "This morning, I think. It wasn't there last night but it was there when I got there after lunch."

"So, sometime this morning. I went over to the clubhouse to open it. I thought it could be parts but it was unmarked. I lifted it and it started beeping. At that point I told everyone to get the fuck out, and here we are."

"Fuck," Nix said. "Do we know it's Fury?"

I nodded. "A few minutes after the explosion I received a call from the Fury's leader, Slade, who confirmed that it was their bomb."

"What are we fuckin' around here for?" Jet asked. "We should go over there and end this, once and for all!"

Nix put a hand on his shoulder. "Easy." He looked at me. "But we should do something. Enough playing nice. You have to see that, now?"

The guys studied me, waiting for my next words.

"Yeah. Like I told Slade. He's declared war."

Jet pumped his fist, the cowboy. He'd probably take them all on himself if we gave him the chance . . . and get his ass shot off in the process.

I held up a hand, my voice rising. "*But* we can't just go in there without our heads on straight just because we're angry and want revenge. We've got to have a plan. I don't want to put any of you at risk if I don't got to. You understand?"

CULLEN

I said this specifically to Jet, who slumped in his seat and frowned. "Okay, so let's make a plan. Let's do this."

Nix shoved him and told him to chill out.

"All right. First," I said, lighting a cigarette and setting it in an ashtray. I clapped my hands together. "What do we got as far as firepower? Did we lose anything in the explosion?"

Nix shook his head. "We haven't been keeping our weapons there. We each have our own stash."

I looked around. "Everyone got their weapons? Ammo?"

Around the room, they nodded.

"All right. So we find out where they are and when they'll be together, and we hit them there."

"Hey," Hart said, lifting his laptop off his knees and turning it to us. "We already know when they'll all be together."

"There was some chatter on one of the phone lines. Something about a surprise birthday party. It was a girl talking to one of Hell's Fury."

"Who and how do you know it was the Fury talking?"

"Who the fuck do you think you're talking to?" Hart put his hands out and smiled a cheeky assed grin. "I hacked in to their phones and I know it was Slade's girl. Roxanne, I think is her name."

"Yeah, Roxanne's definitely Slade's old lady," Zain said.

"It's Slade's birthday," Hart said. "His girl is having a party for him out at the Fury's clubhouse. Tonight."

"Tonight?" I repeated.

"Yeah," Jet said. "Bitch probably doesn't even know what they did. We can hit them when they're drunk and least expecting it."

I'd normally be all in for this kind of retaliation, but something was holding me back. "Well if it's a surprise party, won't their women be there? Innocent people?"

Jet scoffed. "So? We're not after the innocents. And those bitches are far from innocent."

Who are these guys? Was I the only one in the club who thought women and children should be spared from the bullshit that went down between our clubs?

From the looks on their faces, I saw that I was. I'd never noticed before. Never had a reason to, up until now. Before, I probably would've been right with them, with my bloodthirst.

Then Zain looked at me. "You forget what they did to your ex and that little girl?"

I scowled at him. Like I could forget that for a second. And that was the problem, I couldn't.

"It's a good opportunity. When will we get a chance to have them all together like that, where we know where they are?" Ire blazed in my veins as Hart went on, "You know they have church at surprise locations all over the bay. We never know when or where they're going to have it. This could be our best chance."

I went back to the bench, and took a last drag of my cigarette, trying to settle my nerves. Something about this just felt wrong. Too dangerous. Could've been because I'd seen the look in Grace's eyes, heard Ella screaming . . . and now I finally felt like I had something big to lose.

Fuck. A president couldn't feel like this. Once I had something valuable, the whole club was vulnerable. But, I'd almost lost her. And I'd be fucked if I let that happen again. Yeah, I wanted to be careful, safe. But above all, I had to think of my girls.

The men were all looking at me. Eyes thirsty for blood.

And if I didn't fight now, this could go on and on.

If we retaliated now, we could end it, and Grace and Ella would be safe.

"All right," I said, stubbing out the cigarette and nodding. "Grab your weapons, and let's meet here at midnight. And get this done."

Jet and some of the other guys let out a hoot of excitement. I couldn't share it. It'd be nice if this war would end the night it started. But I didn't think that was the case. And these days, I had a lot more to worry about than a few broken windows and a shot-out living room.

As the men filed out, I fisted my hands in my hair but pain sliced through my skull. I wound up tracing my finger over Drake's handiwork. Nix saw me and said, "You okay?"

I nodded, and then frowned. "I don't know. Something feels wrong about this."

"What?" he asked, leaning against the wall. "You know we should've taken them out while we had the chance."

"Yeah." I let out a breath of air and scrubbed my hands over my face. "But you know that once it starts, it ain't gonna end so easy. There will be back and forth. We might just end up wiping each other out."

Nix shrugged. "Yeah. But what's right is right. They started this when they kidnapped an innocent girl."

"And they won't stop. You know they don't play fair. Don't you worry about them getting their hands on Olivia again?" I asked. "She has a target on her back. Yeah, we protect her, but we can only do so much."

Nix gave me a surprised look. "When did you start worrying about that, man? You know our protection's good. And Livvie's all for it. She asks me every day when I get home whether I ripped any new Fury assholes. She's more bloodthirsty than I am."

I let out a low laugh, but it came out broken and uneasy. Grace wasn't bloodthirsty. And I didn't want her to be. I wanted her to have everything she wanted: A normal life.

And I fucking couldn't give it to her.

Chapter Twenty

Grace

I lifted Ella into my arms and carried her out to the cab, waiting at the end of the dark driveway. As I did, I told myself not to cry.

Maybe I'd see Cullen again. Maybe, in another few months, things would calm down, and I could come back. Part of me was also hoping that he'd decide I mattered more than his club, follow after me, and maybe decide to stay with me.

I knew that wouldn't happen. I wasn't stupid. His club was his family, and the Fury had shit all over his family. I wanted him to make them pay. They deserved it.

I just knew I couldn't be around for it.

When I got to the cab at the end of the driveway, I started to open the door. Just then, a car pulled in right behind us, two headlights slashing through the dark, momentarily blinding me. I squinted as the driver's side door opened.

Cullen jumped out, leaving the door open as he came around toward me. "Where do you think you're going?"

I sucked in a breath. "I'm sorry, Cullen, I have to leave."

He moved closer and barred me from the door. "Like hell."

"Cullen . . ."

I stopped as the driver's side door of the cab opened and the driver got out. He waved his cell phone. "Miss. Is this man bothering you?" He eyed Cullen like he was a thug or something.

I shook my head. "No, it's fine."

He eyed me suspiciously as Cullen got in a fighting stance. "Get back in the car, old man," he warned, his eyes flashing to mine.

CULLEN

I rolled my eyes. "Do you really have to be a douche to everyone outside your little circle of friends?" The driver didn't budge, gauging the situation, his finger at the ready to press the emergency button on his phone. "Cullen, please move aside."

I tried to shove him a little, but that was like moving a mountain. It was no contest. He leaned against the door and crossed his arms.

"No. You're staying here. I'm not letting you go again."

I shook my head. "Please Cullen. Let me go. I know you have to stay. I don't blame you. But I can't be here. Ella can't be here. Just . . . be safe, okay? Don't get killed or something."

He lifted off the car and threw his arms up. "Why? Didn't we already go over this? You said you wouldn't leave again. And here you are, leaving."

"You know why. It's too dangerous for Ella."

He started to move aside, his jaw working, a pissed-off expression on his face, when a voice called in the distance. "Grace! Grace! Is that you? Everything okay?"

Cullen whipped his head in the direction of the sound, and I craned my neck over the bulk of his build to see Barry standing at her mailbox, straining to see us in the light. Now Cullen had fire in his eyes and focused on her. "Jesus. Why the fuck is everyone in our business?"

"Maybe if you didn't stop fixing everyone you didn't know with a death-stare, they'd be more friendly?" I asked. Then I called over in a light voice, to show her just how fine everything was. "Everything's fine, Mrs. Sumter."

"Oh, Grace. It's so late. I was worried about you. That poor little baby of yours sure is having a long night. Let us know if you ever need anything!"

"Thank you!" I called over, waving at her. "I've got it under control!" Fuck, I figured child protective services would be paying a visit soon.

CULLEN

"Jesus. They all think I'm trying to kidnap you," he muttered. "In front of my own goddamn house. Come on. Come inside."

I shook my head and stood firm. If I went back in the house with him, my plans of escape would be all over. "No. I'm sorry, Cullen."

His eyes flashed to Ella, sound asleep on my shoulder. "I don't get it. Where do you think you're going anyway?"

"What can't you get, Cullen? I need to get away. You know I'm not safe here. This driver is taking me to L.A."

His eyes narrowed. "L.A.? Where in L.A?"

"I don't know. I thought I'd just find a hotel."

He let out a breath that was partly an ironic laugh. "Since when is that safe? And how will I know when you get there?"

"I'll call you," I told him. "I promise."

He stood there, hands on hips, jaw clenching and unclenching. Then his eyes flashed to the driver and he lifted his hands in surrender. "Back in the car, old man. I'm not touching her. See?"

The old man's eyes volleyed between us, and I nodded. "Tell me when you're ready," he said to me as he slowly slipped back into the cab.

"This isn't right," Cullen muttered, and I saw what was in his mind, as clear as day. The last time I'd skipped out of his life, he hadn't been able to find me. What if I disappeared again?

"I don't have a choice," I said, looking down at Ella. "Especially where she is concerned. You know L.A. will be safer."

"No. I don't know that," he snapped. "Yeah, someplace out of town is probably a good idea. But I'll take you. You understand? I'm not letting you go that easily."

Some where he can keep tabs on me and make sure we don't disappear. I nodded. "Okay."

CULLEN

I turned, opened the door, and looked inside at the driver. "Thank you for waiting. I won't be needing a ride after all."

The man shook his head slowly, his eyes narrowing in the rearview mirror at Cullen. "Aw, sweetheart. You take care of yourself and that little cutie."

I smiled. That was the aim, anyway.

Cullen said, "Let me just change my shirt and we can go."

Cullen took my suitcase out of the cab and put it in the back of the car, an old muscle car from the sixties, a Charger, maybe? It smelled strongly of motor oil, which made me think he must've borrowed it from the garage where he used to work. Cullen went inside, changed out of his bloody shirt, got one of the car seats he'd bought, and fit it into the back of the car.

We fit Ella into the seat and buckled her up, but she barely stirred.

EVIE MONROE

I slid into the front, beside him, as he put his hand on the stick shift and threw the car in reverse. As he did, I saw Barry's form silhouetted in the front door of her house, watching us. She was probably thinking that we were some damn crazy neighbors.

She really only knew the half of it.

Chapter Twenty-One

Cullen

I threw Hart's old Charger into reverse and sped down the hill, noticing how our neighbor was watching us like a hawk. I started to roll down the window before I realized it might be too much air for Ella. I let out a breath and turned up the fan, but foul-smelling, dank air filled the cabin. "Really happy you made best friends with that old bat so that she can keep tabs on us, everywhere we go."

She rolled her eyes at me. "Would you stop being an asshole every two seconds?"

"As long as you stop being absolutely fucking ridiculous," I muttered at her. "You know I like my privacy."

"No. I know you're pathetically antisocial unless it's a Cobra or a hot girl."

I frowned at her as I pulled up to the stoplight near the Circle K, on the road leading out of town.

EVIE MONROE

She bit her lip and studied a sign that said, SANTA BARBARA 30 mi. "How far away is L.A.?"

I shrugged. "Too far."

L.A. I wasn't fucking going to L.A. I'd tucked my piece in the back of my jeans, had another one in my boot. I was prepared for war. What I was going to do was get about a half-hour out of town, drop her and Ella at the swankiest place I could find in the nicest neighborhood, and then high-tail it up to Aveline Bay to discuss our little party with the Fury.

She looked at me. It was like she could read my mind, the suspicion in her voice. "Where are you taking me?"

"Like I said. Somewhere safe."

She tapped on her lips. "Out of town?"

I nodded.

She yawned. "Okay. What happened at church?"

I gave her a look. She knew better than to ask me that. What happened there, stayed there. I didn't take chances. Though I knew I could probably trust her. "We just have to get you somewhere safe."

"And then you're going back to deal with it?" She cocked her head at me.

"I've got to."

"So you're just going to go back and shoot them all up and get yourself killed in the process?"

I pressed my lips together. "That's not the plan."

She sighed and leaned her head against the door. "Yeah, but it could happen. And eventually, one day, it will."

"All right," I said, my voice rising. "Maybe it will. But let's not talk about that, okay?"

I didn't want to sound on edge, but I knew I wasn't doing a good job of it. Right now, the Cobras were getting locked and loaded, preparing for an all out war, and I should've been leading the charge. But, I was here getting Grace and Ella squared away. I checked the time on my phone. It was after ten. Once I got her settled at the hotel, I'd need to high-tail it back to Aveline Bay to be there by midnight.

As I turned onto Route One, my phone in the cup holder lit up. I craned my neck to see a message from Zain.

I picked up the phone and read: *Midnight, right?*

I shoved the phone down into the cup holder. Zain never listened that well. As I was shoving it down, the phone lit up again, and there was another message, from Hart.

I picked up the phone and read that text: *Definitely a blowout going on over at their clubhouse. Just went by.*

Fuck. My pulse pounded. I wanted to ask him if he saw any sign of Slade there, but I couldn't. I was driving, and I got the feeling Grace was sitting beside me, quietly giving me the stink-eye. I glanced over at her, and sure enough . . . she was.

When my phone lit up again and I reached for it, she said, "You know, you do have Ella in the back seat so you might want to, I don't know, keep your eyes on the road?"

I scowled at her and raked my hair out of my eyes. "Hey, baby, it's all good."

"I really don't want to end this night swimming in the Pacific," she muttered, then hissed, "*Keep that fucking phone out of your hand.*"

I saluted her in response, but I wasn't in the mood to get into one of our good old-fashioned screaming matches.

We drove in silence for the next ten minutes, though every ten seconds, my phone lit up with a new message. I was the commander of this assault, and I'd gone AWOL. I knew the guys were probably going batshit crazy, like they always did without me. I sucked in a breath when we got just outside of Santa Barbara and I pulled into a hotel overlooking the ocean.

"Good?" I asked her, pulling into the roundabout and cutting the engine.

EVIE MONROE

She looked up at it and wrinkled her nose. I think anything I picked wouldn't be good enough for her, just because I'd picked it.

"Well, it's not the Best Western, but . . ." I said with a chuckle.

A valet jogged up to us and opened the front doors. "Hello and welcome to . . ." The guy looked me over and cleared his throat. "The Vanderbilt Ocean Resort. Checking in?"

I nodded and handed him the keys. "She and the kid are. But I got the bags. Just park this somewhere for me."

I reached into the trunk and pulled out her suitcase. The valet, in his bow tie and jacket, looked us over like he wasn't sure if we were lost. Grace was in these little short-shorts that probably were forbidden in a place like this, and my body was still covered in a thin layer of grime from the explosion, not to mention that I wasn't this place's normal clientele. A man and a woman walked by in evening dress, gaping at us, as the valet asked, "Do you have reservations?"

CULLEN

I shook my head, reached into my wallet, and pulled out a hundred, which I handed to him. "Take good care of it. Okay?"

He nodded eagerly. "Yes, sir. Right away, sir."

I put the suitcase on the curb as Grace finished unsnapping Ella from her car seat. She was awake now, her head whipping around to take in the new sights.

Grace looked around as we went through the revolving doors, her eyes wide. "Um, Cullen?" she asked, pulling on the sleeve of my T-shirt. "I would've been fine with a motel on the side of the road."

I gave her a look. "There's no way."

She nodded, conceding that that idea of hers had been a fucking terrible one, and followed me across the vast lobby, past crystal chandeliers, over shining marble floors and deep oriental rugs, with clusters of expensive leather sofas and tufted chairs arranged in tight circles. When we got to the check-in desk, the woman there raised an eyebrow at us. "Can I help you?"

I approached the desk and drummed my fingers on the counter. "Yeah. Checking in." I looked at Grace, trying to see inside her mind to what she was thinking, then at Ella. "You have a crib?"

The woman regarded me. "We do have playpens and cribs available. But first I need some information. Do you have a reservation?"

I shook my head. "Nope."

She pressed her lips together and typed something into her computer. "I'm sorry, sir. But we're fully booked for the night. It *is* a Friday."

Shit. "Seriously? You don't . . . you know. Hold rooms back or anything? For like, celebrities?"

She raised an eyebrow. She'd probably be hot, if she wasn't so stuck up. "I'm sorry."

I gave her my most charming smile. "So you're telling me that if the president of the United States showed up at this place, you would turn him away?"

She smiled. "Well . . . no. We have our Warner Bungalow suite, actually. It's the owner's private suite.

CULLEN

It's two-thousand square feet, comes with a private entrance and private twenty-foot heated pool hot tub, private balcony, private patio with fountain."

I held a hand up. "That's it. We'll take it."

Her smile faltered when she realized I was serious. "I'm sorry, I can't do that."

"Why not? Is it currently occupied?"

She shook her head. "Well, no, but—"

"Then what's the problem? The woman's really tired. She'd like to get some shut-eye."

She drew in a breath and let it go in a rush. "I'm sorry, sir. But the Warner Bungalow is five-thousand dollars a night."

"Don't be sorry, baby," I said to her. I reached into my pocket and pulled out a wad of cash and counted out five thousand dollars in hundred dollar bills, which I pushed over to her. "This'll cover it?"

She nodded, astonished. Then she quickly typed something into her little computer. "If you'll wait just a moment, I'll have a porter come to escort you to your room and set up your bags. He'll show you around the suite and deliver a complimentary bottle of champagne." She pushed the key over to us.

"No thanks. We can find the room on our own. We're not into the bubbly. Just tell me where it is."

The receptionist gave me a wide-eyed stare and said, "You can take that corridor behind you to the room. It's on the beach side." From her tone of voice, I think she was glad to be rid of us.

"Great," I said, memorizing the directions. "Can you have a crib delivered?" I scooped up the keys and cocked an imaginary hat at her. "Thanks a lot."

When I turned around, Grace was staring at me with a look that could kill. "What?" I said, striding into the corridor.

"Were you flirting with that woman? Really? While I was right there?"

CULLEN

I grinned at her. "Baby. You always said I need to be a little friendlier to strangers. That's what I'm doing. What, are you jealous?"

She screwed up her face. "Of what?"

I patted my chest proudly. "That chick was totally into me."

She scoffed. "Please."

"Hey. Think what you want. Got us the last room in the place, didn't it?"

She scowled at me. "Yeah, I think your thousands of dollars might have gotten you that room. Not your charm or that hot bod of yours."

I shrugged. "What difference does it make? It's not like I was going to do her. I have you and the kid. That doesn't exactly make me a chick magnet."

Her jaw dropped in disgust.

"Don't give me that, sweetheart. You're not sleeping in a fleabag motel room on the side of the road. You might want to thank me?"

She rolled her eyes and hefted Ella higher on her hip as we went outside, to a path trailing down to the beach. I followed the darkened corridor of jungle plants to the bungalow at the very end of the path and inserted the key card into the slot.

I pushed open the door and stepped aside to let her go in.

Grace walked in and scanned the room, a giant great room with modern furnishings. If she was impressed, you wouldn't know it. She looked more annoyed than anything else. Ella started to squirm in her arms so she set her on the ground and let out a big sigh.

"What, princess? This ain't good enough for you and your superior tastes?" I said.

"It's fine. I just wish you wouldn't do that. Throwing your money around like some kind of pimp. It's embarrassing," she muttered. "And it makes everyone uncomfortable. Including me."

CULLEN

I stared at her. "Excuse me? You have a problem with me?"

"Yeah. You heard me. They probably look at you, wondering what bank you knocked over," she says with a flip of her hair, revealing the bird tattoo she'd gotten years ago. "And it doesn't impress me, that's for sure. You look like a thug who has too much money he doesn't know what to do with."

"Baby, I don't give a shit what anyone thinks. And I've given up trying to impress you." I strode through the giant bungalow, which was more like a house, checking things out. The place was decent. I'd been here before, with my dad, long ago. Someone like Grace, who didn't grow up with this shit, should've been impressed.

But leave it to Grace to walk around the place, looking like she hated it all.

Someone knocked on the door, and I went to open it. It was housekeeping, delivering the crib. I thanked and tipped them, then rolled it in. "Where do you want it?"

She sighed. Then she pointed to a corner of the living room. "I guess . . . put it over there."

I did as she said, then checked my phone. I had no less than twelve text messages from different guys. I needed to be at the meeting. I quickly started to thumb in a message to Nix to tell him that I'd be late when I looked up and saw Grace gazing at me.

Not with anything close to appreciation. No, she still looked pissed. "Let me guess. Cobras business. Morning, noon, and night?"

I let out a huff of air. What did she expect from me? Our club had just taken an ass-whipping like we'd never seen. I should've been out doing damage control. Instead, I'd taken time out of my Cobras business to get her someplace safe. I'd holed her up in a nice piece of real estate on the fucking beach with a freaking heated pool and a hot tub. And now she was giving me shit because I was trying to send a couple messages to my guys to tell them I'd be a while?

Un-fucking-believable.

CULLEN

I opened my mouth to put her in her place when she tossed her hair again, baring that tattoo of the birds. And suddenly it occurred to me what really had me on edge.

She'd been trying to run away again. In that cab. Without a note or a message to me, to tell me where she was going.

And she could easily do it, even now, the second I got my ass back to Aveline Bay. Tomorrow, she could get an Uber and disappear for another two years. For a lifetime. I didn't know.

So I bit my tongue. "Baby," I said. "Why don't you get yourself to bed?"

She snorted. "Because I *have* a baby. Remember? Ella?"

I watched as she set Ella down on the couch, changed her diaper, and pushed her legs and arms into a one-piece jumper thing. Then she set up the blankets in the bottom of the crib and lifted her up and into the crib. "I hope she can sleep here," she said, gnawing on her lip. "She liked the big girl bed at your house."

But Ella road tested the crib, jumping a few times, before she dropped down and closed her eyes. She gnawed on her little thumb, and before Grace had covered her with a blanket, she was out like a light.

Then Grace went into the big bedroom, ignoring the super-size bed and made a dash for the bathroom and showered. I sat on the couch overlooking the ocean and thought about the fucked up war with the Fury. Fuck. Three weeks ago I wouldn't have had a second thought about fucking them up.

I'm the goddamn president of the Cobras, and I'm having second thoughts? I need to get my goddamn head on straight.

When I heard the bathroom door open I tiptoed into the bedroom so I wouldn't wake Ella, maybe I was getting good at this dad thing. Grace came out and had changed into a pair of boxers and tank top and had her wet hair wrapped in a towel.

CULLEN

"*Now*, are you going to sleep?" I asked her.

She shook her head. "I'm a little wired. I think I'll go out to the patio and get some air." She looked at me. "Is that okay? You don't think they'll . . ."

"Nah," I said, thinking of the so-called party at the Fury's clubhouse. I felt confident she'd be safe for tonight. What had worried me most was getting her out of town, unseen. Now that she was out, I felt good about it. Like they were in the right place.

What I didn't feel so good about was my club. Prepping for war without me. All kinds of things could happen if I wasn't there to back them up. And if anything bad went down, I'd have no one to blame but myself.

I needed something to calm my nerves. I went to the mini bar across from the bed and grabbed all the little bottles of Jack I could find. I downed the first one, tossed it in the trash, and followed her outside, unscrewing the top of the second one.

It was a nice patio, with smooth stone pavers, lounge chairs and a hot tub. An entrance from the living room and the bedroom. A fountain burbled in the center. She walked around the high-walled perimeter, bordered with vegetation, taking it all in, then reached down at the side of the pool and felt the water. The clouds of earlier had pushed off and now the night was kind of sultry. This private patio . . . and Grace, wearing her barely-there clothes, her nipples visible through her tight-white T, would've been a grand opportunity, any other day of my life.

Right now, it was hell. I needed to get out. I polished off the second bottle of Jack, sat down on a chair outside and drummed my fingers on my knees.

After her little tour of the patio, she eyed the empty bottle, then me, suspiciously. "If you have somewhere to be, don't let me keep you."

Right. There was nothing keeping me. I needed to get back.

CULLEN

But there *was* something keeping me. I wanted to keep her with me at all times. I didn't want to lose her again.

"You'll stay here? In this room?" I asked her, standing. "Until I get back?"

She nodded, still surveying the patio.

That wasn't enough for me. "Will you?"

"Yes," she said absently, pushing a lounge chair closer to the pool. I couldn't be sure she was listening to me.

I said, louder: "Hey. Will you?"

"For the last time, yes!" she snapped, tossing her ponytail. "Damn. Thanks, warden. I told you I'd be here, and I'll be here. Fuck! It's not like I have anywhere else to go."

Anger bubbled inside me. How the fuck could she blame me for asking, when she'd done it before? "That never stopped you before," I ground out.

She scowled at me. "Please just leave. Maybe then I can have some peace."

"Peace? Really? You're a piece of work," I growled at her.

She came up close to me and wagged a finger in my face. "If it weren't for you, I wouldn't have had to leave Aveline Bay in the first place!"

"Yeah? Well, if it weren't for you, maybe I wouldn't be on the border of complete insanity, baby," I muttered. I checked the pockets for the keys to the car, until I remembered I'd left them with the valet. I turned to go. "I'm leaving."

"Good," she muttered, not looking at me. She was staring at the pool.

I clenched my fists, then gave her double middle fingers behind her back.

I turned to go. As I slid the patio door opened, I looked back and watched as she reached for the bottom hem of her shirt and pulled it up over her head, baring her back.

CULLEN

I stood there, staring as she reached for the waistband of her boxers. "What the fuck are you doing?"

She peered over her shoulder at me. "Oh, goody. You're still here," she mumbled, mock-excited. "What does it look like I'm doing?"

Swimming, partly. But mostly, teasing the shit out of me, getting my cock as hard as a rock. I don't think she meant to do it. I think she really wanted me gone. But if that was what she wanted, this was definitely the wrong way to go about it.

I stood there, my hand on the door, unable to tear my eyes away. "You going in there like that?"

She nodded, pulled on the waistband, and let her shorts fall in a puddle at her feet. "Don't own a bathing suit. And the water is so nice. I just wanted to swim a little."

I watched her walk toward the pool, dipping her toe in. Mesmerized. I knew there was something I was trying to get back to in Aveline Bay, something important, an appointment or some shit like that, but I lost all focus when she slipped beneath the water and came out, pushing her wet hair back from her face, all dark now with water, and looked over at me.

Her words told me to get the fuck out, but her eyes told me to stay.

Fuck it. Fuck me. Fuck everything.

I closed the patio door and moved toward her. "I thought you had somewhere to be?" she asked, looking up at me.

I shook my head slowly.

She shrugged, then pushed back in a backstroke, her perfect tits bobbing on the surface of the water. Her eyes never leaving mine. I watched her, doing long, slow strokes, every movement playing my cock like a guitar. And she knew it. She knew exactly what she was doing to me.

With a glance in my direction, she climbed out of the pool, went to the hot tub, turned it on, and slipped into the bubbling water. Then she leaned back, closed her eyes, and said, "If you're not joining me, then leave."

I didn't have to be asked twice. I walked to the edge of the hot tub, leaned over her, and captured her mouth in mine.

And the second my mouth met hers, I knew it.

There was no way I could bring myself to leave her again.

EVIE MONROE

CULLEN

Chapter Twenty-Two

Grace

There was always something so primal, so savage about the way Cullen kissed. At first, he just licked at the seam of my lips, priming me for what was to come. He nibbled on my lips, just slightly, getting a taste.

And then he dove in to taste me, all-in. Wet. Hot. Hungrier than I'd ever seen him.

He explored my mouth with his tongue as he did everything, demanding, and sexy as hell. He tasted of Jack and cigarettes, but most of all, like *him*, a taste I couldn't get enough of. He groaned, pushing deeper. The wet heat of his mouth was enough to unravel me completely.

And once we started, there was no turning back.

He ripped his lips from mine for a split second, pulling his shirt off his back and revealing his rock-hard chest, that effortlessly magnificent six-pack. He unbuttoned and unzipped his fly, reaching behind his back and pulling out a gun, which I thought he might have been trying to hide from me.

I didn't care. I knew he had it. I'd seen the bulge behind his back before. I understood what had been on his mind, and the mind of all the Cobras, tonight. Revenge. I could see it in the way he moved, so tense and uptight, that he was planning for big things. Dangerous things.

It wasn't that I was trying to keep him safe, to stop him from running into a war zone.

Okay, maybe it was part of it. I'd seen what the Fury could do, and it scared the hell out of me.

But a bigger part of it was that I just needed him here. I didn't want to be alone.

Cullen usually had a grace, a smoothness, a cocky slowness to which he did everything. But this time, even he looked a little over-excited. He kicked off his big boots, then sat down and slipped out of his jeans. He shed the rest of his clothes in record timing, slipped into the water, and pulled me to him, his hot mouth finding mine again.

I ran my hands down the hard planes of his body, feeling hot and feverish as he scooped me up and sat me onto his lap, straddling his muscular thighs. He looked up at me in the misty air, pushing the wet ropes of hair from my face. His voice was breathy. "You can't do that to me, baby. Don't tease me like that."

The way he acted sometimes, like a big cocky asshole, he begged to be teased. The problem was, he was mostly immune to that kind of magic.

But not now.

Oh, definitely not now.

His heavy-lidded eyes, moving from my nose, to my cheeks, to my chin, like a kid in a candy store deciding which part of me he wanted to have first, his breath coming in ragged bursts, his heavily beating heart . . . it all told me that without a doubt, he'd fallen under my spell.

He clenched his teeth and let out a roar of pure, raw masculinity as I spread my legs on his thighs and pressed my pubes against his cock. It pulsed in response, alive, eager. God, I loved his thick cock. "Like how?"

His hands dipped under the water, kneading my ass hard, digging his fingers into my flesh. I rubbed my pained nipples up and down on his chest, wanting more. "You know," he growled.

I gave him an innocent bat of the eyelashes, and he dug in harder in response, pulling me to him, until his dick was sandwiched between us.

I leaned over and took his earlobe between my teeth, flicking it with my tongue. "You ever take a woman in a hot tub?"

I knew the answer to that. He had a hot tub in his backyard, so yes. Probably often, since this was the great Cullen McKnight. This was my first time ever even sitting in a hot tub, and I liked it. I liked the warmth of the water, flushing our skin, the gentle massaging of the bubbles . . . but most of all I liked him, naked and under my thighs, his hard, wet body pressed against mine.

And I intended to make my virgin experience in a hot tub one we'd both always remember.

I would've told him that, but he was now a man possessed, and the last thing he seemed interested in was talking. One hand roved up my back, tangled in the hair at the nape of my neck, and pulled. He positioned me right where he wanted me, trailing the hottest of kisses down my body. My collarbone, my chest, between my breasts.

Then, taking my breast in one hand, he fastened his mouth on the nipple and bit down so hard that I cried out. The bite became a fierce suck, and I let out a moan, the feeling firing straight to my clit, making me squirm against him.

"Easy, baby," he murmured against my skin, lapping at both nipples with his tongue, one after the other. Sucking and tasting them so thoroughly I thought I'd go insane.

"I can't," I breathed out, my cunt aching, my blood pulsing through my body like thunder. "Please."

Now, he was the one teasing me, lavishing attention on my boobs as I tried to squirm on him, getting his cock where I wanted it to go. I rubbed myself on him, nudging him where I wanted him to be, but he was fully intent on bringing me to the edge of insanity. This went on forever, and not long enough at the same time.

He stopped, lifted his head, staring deeply into my eyes. He pressed his forehead against mine, his powerful chest rising as those brilliant blue eyes penetrated right to my core. "You're mine."

"Yes," I said, begging. Pleading. "Yes. All yours."

His hand fell under the water again, between us, and he lifted his cock up. "All right, baby," he said, motioning me with his chin. I lifted up on my knees and felt him there, where I needed him to be, at the entrance of my pussy. He pressed his hardness against me, letting me feel everything he could give me. "Ride me."

CULLEN

He exhaled. I inhaled in anticipation, ready to feel every inch of him as I slid onto him.

Then he wound his hands around my waist and slammed me down, hard, onto his waiting cock, a defiant look in his eyes that made me gasp out all the air in my lungs.

The feeling of complete and perfect connection was too much. Nothing could compare to this. I needed to move on him, to feel more. But he kept his hands on my hips, holding me to him.

"That's where you belong, Grace. Right here. You're not getting away again," he ground out, his eyes never leaving mine. "I'll follow you to the ends of the earth if I have to."

I touched his face, his jaw. "You let me go before."

"Biggest mistake I ever made. I won't make it again."

"What changed? Ella?"

His large hands cupped my face, and he kissed me again, rasping against my mouth, "It's you. It's always been you. I was too stupid to realize it before. What you mean to me."

I started to move up and down on him, now, and he helped me along, holding my hips, moving me in a slow, sweet rhythm. I rocked my hips in time with his, in that perfect synchronicity, trading breath as we panted together. His gaze locked on mine as he kissed my mouth, then he dipped his head and gently bit my neck, his warm, uneven breath making me arch my back to get closer to him. His hand trailed between my legs and his thumb found my clit.

I dragged my hands down the contours of his back, feeling each sinewy, perfect muscle as he strained against the back of the tub. My fingers raked through his hair, feeling the raised line of the ragged scar where he'd been sewn up. Where he'd been hurt, protecting me.

Protecting us.

The thought of that made me want to give him more, give him everything of me. All of it. I tilted my pelvis to get closer, sending fireworks of pleasure through my body as he plunged in deeper. I tilted my head to the sky and my eyes rolled back into my head.

"You feel so good, Grace. So fucking good," he breathed out. "Come on, baby. Come for me."

I started to move faster still, more erratically, until I felt myself breaking apart, into a thousand pieces, swallowing a scream as he joined me in release, gripping my hips harder and jerking in violent convulsions. I closed my eyes and saw stars in the back of my eyelids.

"God, you're so fucking beautiful," he murmured, his breath shuddery, coaxing me down for a kiss. Winding his hand through my hair again, he said, "You're the only one who's ever mattered. You know that?"

I did. In Cullen's eyes, most of the world could just fuck off, but the people he cared about? It was impossible for them not to know. I could feel his love in everything, in the way he held me in his strong arms, in the way he kissed me, the way he gazed at me with a reverence he had for nothing and nobody else.

But he couldn't say it. I didn't know if he'd ever said those words to anyone. I'd had my mother, my grandmother long ago, and Ella, now. He'd never had a soul. I wasn't afraid to say the words now, even if he wouldn't return in kind, because I knew he felt it. And I'd rather have the actions than the words. I gazed into his eyes, and whispered, "I love you, too, Cullen."

He let out a breath, laid his head on my shoulder, and held me tight against the wall of his chest. I could feel his heart beat in time with mine. We just stayed there, locked together, content.

When I finally pulled myself off him, I said, "Are you going to leave?"

He slipped down lower into the hot tub and looked up at the sky. "Hell, no. I'm right where I need to be."

I smiled. "Good."

"You know that day? The one on the beach?" he asked me suddenly, as he wrapped his strong arm around me.

CULLEN

I did. It was the day he'd told me he was so lucky to have me, the day I thought I'd have something different than my mother ever had. The day I'd started to believe in love. "Yeah."

"I told you I was lucky because I had you," he said. "I still believe that. Without you, my whole world turned to shit."

"But you still became president."

He scoffed. "Being president is nothing. When you left . . . yeah, I tried to fill my life with it. But something was always fucking missing. And now I've found it. That's why I don't want to let you go."

I leaned my head against his shoulder as he kissed my forehead. "You don't have to worry, Cullen. I said I left because I was afraid you'd tell me to get rid of the baby. But really, I left because I didn't want to be like my mother."

"Your . . . mother?" he asked, confusion in his voice. "You never told me about her."

"I don't talk about her. She wanted a man to love her so bad. I was only a kid and I knew how desperate she was. I remembered all the men she invited into the house, and every one of them was worse than the next. My mother was beautiful and had so many admirers. They all wanted her. But what they didn't want? A kid. Some of them hit me, abused me emotionally. She didn't know, because I kept it quiet. I just wanted her to be happy, and I saw how happy those men made her. But when I was fourteen, she found one of them in bed with me, raping me."

He's silent, but I could hear his jaw working, his teeth grinding.

"She was so beside herself, thinking she'd failed me, that she killed herself before I turned fifteen."

He winced.

"I just didn't want to be her. Trying to be with men who don't want to be a father. I thought I'd rather do it alone. And I tried to, until it became too hard and I was faced with living out on the streets with Ella."

CULLEN

He tucked a finger under my chin and lifted my head so he could stare into my eyes. "Baby, I'm sorry. I'm so fucking sorry I ever made you doubt me. I want you. I want Ella."

He kissed me lightly on the lips, his hand skimming down my side. As the fingers of his other hand lightly stroked the side of my face, his eyes searched mine, brilliant in their intensity, blue as the hottest flame.

We sat in the tub for a while longer, mostly silent, until our skin was beyond pruned. After that, he got out, wrapped a fluffy hotel towel around his hips, and lifted me out. He sat me on the lounge and proceeded to wipe me down with a pile of towels . . . one for each body part, I think. Cullen wasn't big on eco-friendliness.

"I feel like a pampered princess," I told him, as he lifted each of my legs and wiped the water droplets off. He was extremely thorough, his callused hands finding their way over every inch of my skin, making me hot for him again. Then he wrapped me in a big, fluffy robe. "Maybe you should fan me and feed me grapes."

"Don't push your luck," he said, but his lips were twisted up in a wry smile.

I could get used to this, I thought as he carried me inside and placed me in the center of the bed like a flower. But I had something to do first and pushed away from him.

I crept into the living room to peek into Ella's crib. She was still sound asleep and hadn't even budged from the position she'd been in before. I hurried back into the bedroom, resisting when he tried to lure me into joining him under the big, soft cloud of the comforter. "I should probably take a shower," I whispered.

"You already did," he said, pulling me to him and draping his arm over me. He drew me close to him and kissed my wet hair. His hand roamed under my robe, between my legs. "I can't get enough of you."

CULLEN

He pulled on the tie of my robe, exposing me to him, and his eyes roved over my body, glinting like it was a feast he couldn't wait to devour. Whatever inhibitions I had disappeared I saw such lust-filled desire in his eyes.

He reached over and propped a pillow under my head. He spread my legs and knelt between them, then grabbed me by the ass, dragged my lower half up, to his waiting prick. I lifted up, grabbing for him, raking my hands down his back as he pulled me onto his cock. He started to fuck me, hard and fast, like an animal, and I lost everything. All sense of where we were, who I was, what we were running from . . . it all went out the window as he dipped his face down to mine, feeding me his tongue.

"Oh," I murmured, wondering how it was that he could make me feel this good. Make me lose it, like no one else ever had. Every one of my nerve-endings was alive, singing. I tightened my arms around his neck. My nipples hardening, my belly swimming, I felt my body ratcheting up for another orgasm, even more unbelievable than the last one. His hands held my breasts, the pads of his thumbs flicking over the nipples, and all the while he kept a frantic rhythm, his hips meeting mine, claiming me, dragging moan after moan from my throat.

When I went off, he was right there with me, in perfect sync. I came in a way I never had before, so hard and exquisitely. The warmth that filled me was so satisfying and sweet that I couldn't imagine anything better.

Because for the first time, I felt really, truly wanted.

He tilted his head up, listening for Ella in the next room as he pulled out of me. "Still asleep. Despite your noise."

I scrunched my nose. "*My* noise? What about you?"

He grinned and fell back onto the mattress, blinking. Then said, "Wow. I am beat."

CULLEN

The next thing I knew, his breathing had slowed. I rolled over and put my chin on his chest, watching his eyelids twitching.

The bastard had fallen asleep. Who knew, getting into a turf war with another motorcycle club and nearly dying would've tuckered the poor baby out?

I let out a little laugh. Despite all the hard muscles, his pectorals rippling with tattoos, he looked so uncharacteristically boyish, sleeping there with nothing but that towel slung across his waist. Looking at him like this, with his thick half-moon of eyelashes, his pink lips, he just looked so pretty, it was hard to believe he was the head of a motorcycle gang. I leaned over and set a hand on his big bare shoulder, the warmth of which seeped into me and I kissed his forehead. He smelled like chlorine and Jack, a heady mixture that had me wanting him all over again.

God, he'd turned me into a sex addict, one of those people who'd happily lie in bed all day, waiting for it.

EVIE MONROE

I slipped off the bed, pulling off the robe, and went to take another quick shower to get the chlorine out of my hair.

Five minutes later, I returned, and peeked at the bed to see him completely still, sleeping. God, he was sexy, his nakedness and the way his cock slightly tented the towel making me wet again. I wanted to strip off the towel and lie beside him, run my hands over his muscled legs, his narrow hips, his thick, long cock, up his washboard abs to the most perfect chest I'd ever seen. Even now, it was hard to believe the things we'd done, and all that beautiful work of art had been inside me.

I changed into a tank and boxers, and watched him sleep for a little while, watched his smooth, chest rising and falling in the moonlight coming through the sliding glass door. I thought of what he'd have been doing, otherwise, tonight. Cullen took risks, he always had. Would tonight have been the risk that could've ended his life?

CULLEN

Thinking of that, I remembered the gun, which was still lying outside by the hot tub. I went out and picked up his dirty clothes, his boots, all the while staring at the gun.

I swallowed. I'd held it before, once, while we'd been playing around in bed. I'd joked around, asking if it made me look badass and sexy. He hadn't thought it was funny, but it took me some time to figure out why. He wasn't trying to *look* like a badass.

He was a badass and with his lifestyle, he needed that gun to survive.

I carefully lifted it up, holding it like some infected thing, and then grabbed for his heavy boots. They were super-heavy, and when I peeked inside, I figured out why. He had another gun in one of them.

Jesus. He hadn't just wanted revenge. He was going for another wild west shootout, just like the one that he'd said had been at his house.

This was the life that I could expect with Cullen.

But I hoped to God Ella would forgive me if anything ever happened. Because I'd never be able to leave him now.

When I set his things on the dresser, I stared at the guns. I thought about locking it in the closet safe, but decided against it, so I just put it in the top drawer.

I realized how dry my throat was. I crept over to the mini-bar to check it out, but all I could find were sodas and a few remaining bottles of alcohol, since Cullen had cleaned out almost everything else. What I really wanted was some plain old water. I'd seen a vending machine on our way to the bungalow, so I figured I could get something, then be back in a few minutes. Reaching into my purse, I found a couple of dollar bills.

I opened the door to the suite and walked along the secluded jungle pathway and soon caught sight of the glowing display of the vending machine.

Suddenly, the roar of motorcycles startled me. More than just one. It sounded like several, maybe a whole army. And it also sounded like they were close, maybe right in the parking lot.

I didn't know much about Cullen's club, but I did know that the Vanderbilt probably wasn't a place for bikers. In fact, I was pretty sure that was why Cullen had chosen this place for me. To keep me away from the Fury.

I froze. My heart jammed itself in my throat.

Crumpling the dollar bills into my hand, I whirled around and ran as fast as I could, back to the bungalow.

EVIE MONROE

Chapter Twenty-Three

Cullen

I'd been having a dream. In it, I was somewhere far away from Aveline Bay, and I felt happy. It was just me and Grace, her naked body pressed up against me. It was nothing but warm, perfect paradise. The sun was shining on our faces and we had no cares in the world. Everything was so damn good.

"Cullen," her sweet voice whispered playfully in my ear, rousing me. "Cullen."

I rolled over and took her in my arms, drawing her soft lips against mine, but instead of kissing me, she said, louder, more urgently, "Cullen!"

I woke with a start to see Grace over me in the darkness, her eyes wide as moons. Her hair was wet and she was dressed. Moonlight slashed through the window. It couldn't have been morning yet. I tried to sit up. "What time is it?"

"After two." Her voice trembled, and her hands shook. She was holding something in her hands. A crumpled dollar bill. "I think they're here."

I scrubbed a hand over my face. "Who?"

"Who's here?"

"I was thirsty so I went outside to get some water from the vending machine."

"You went outside?" My voice rose.

"Well, yes. You said . . ."

Damn, I should have told her that going outside, at this hour of the night, anyone could have grabbed her. She had no idea what kind of chance she'd been taking. The Fury were everywhere, and their numbers had always been larger than ours. I'd been playing it too safe when I told her I wasn't worried. "Forget what I said," I told her, as suddenly, it hit me.

It was after two. And I was supposed to meet the rest of the Cobras at midnight.

CULLEN

I'd abandoned my club. I swung my head around the room, looking for my phone. I found it on the night stand and lifted it up, checking my messages.

The screen was on fire. More than twenty different messages from the guys, all versions of "where the fuck are you?"

Grace had started pacing frantically, chewing on a fingernail. I stood up and got in her path, dragging her hand from her mouth. "All right. What did you see?"

"I heard it. A whole bunch of motorcycles. Out by the main building."

I dropped her hand to look for my clothes. She brought it right back up to her mouth and started chewing. She'd piled my clothing on the dresser. I tossed aside the towel and shimmied into my jeans, looking for my weapon. "Gun?"

She motioned to the drawer. I opened it and slid my gun into my waistband, while I scanned the rest of the space around me. The closet was filled with the basics, Grace's luggage and crap for Ella, extra pillows, room to hang clothes. I moved things around and said, "Do me a favor. Get Ella and hide in here."

"Why? You think . . ."

"I just think you'll be safer in there. It's probably nothing. Just some passing bikers," I said, even though I doubted it.

She moved into the living room, quietly scooped Ella into her arms and ran back into the bedroom, moving past me, into the closed space. I leaned down and kissed the worried wrinkle on her forehead. "Hey. No problem. It'll be fine."

She nodded and pulled Ella to her chest, then sank down to the floor of the closet as I closed the door. Taking my phone, I jabbed in a text to Hart: *What's going on?*

I went to the sliding glass door and peered out, but all it did was provide a view of the high-walled courtyard. Everything looked fine out there. What I couldn't see was the outside the bungalow. There were no windows facing the front of the resort. A second later, I saw a text from Hart: *Yo. Where you at?*

I answered: *Long story. What's going on now?*

I watched the three dots, indicating he was typing back, all the while dragging my eyes up to the front door. This could all be a mistake. The Fury were having a party. They hadn't seen us leave town. The Vanderbilt was just off the Pacific Coast Highway, a nice ride. What Grace heard outside could've just been a bunch of bikers out for a nighttime joyride.

Hart came back with: *We waited until 12:30 and then Nix made the call that we should go on without you. But it was a front. We got there and the Fury had cleared out.*

My body tensed. I thumbed in, *Vanderbilt Resort* as a loud banging shook the front door. I reached back for my piece, then pressed SEND and pocketed my phone, cocking my gun. If Hart was the genius he said he was, he'd figure it out if I didn't respond. I pointed the barrel right at the door, taking a step forward.

"Yeah?" I called. "Who is it?"

"Cullen, buddy!" a voice said. For fuck's sake. Bruiser, the VP of the Fury. "It's your old friend. Let us in."

Bruiser and I went way back. He was about forty-five and as crass an asshole as you could imagine, plus he was dumb as a stump. It was a miracle he'd made it to VP in the first place. I'd had run-ins with him about half a dozen times over the years, and during the last one, he'd nearly killed his girlfriend trying to run me down on his bike in a parking lot. She'd been hopping on the back of his bike and he'd gunned it, coming after me. A Fury through and through; all they ever did was think about themselves.

"What the fuck do you want?" I called out.

I could sense that smug smile on his fat-ass face. "I think you know."

I raked my hand through my hair, feeling the raised S-shape of the stitching Drake had given me. "No, I don't. How about you tell me? How the hell'd you find me, anyway? Can't a man get out of town for a weekend?"

"Well, Cullen. You know how much interest we take in you." He let out a loud, gravelly laugh. "While all your minions were preparing to break up our party, we were watching you. We've got friends all over, keeping tabs on you and that tasty slut of yours. By the way, why weren't you with your club? That tasty little whore of yours too good to pass up?"

I threw my head to the ceiling and let out a sigh. Fuck. It'd be a good half-hour before Hart and the guys got over here. "What do you want?"

"Oh, we've got a lot to talk about. But it'll be a lot easier if you open the door and we do it face to face."

Hell fucking no. Not with my girls here. I for sure as hell didn't want to see Bruiser's ugly mug in the same place as them. "Over my dead body."

"You want us to knock the door down? Don't think we're just going to go away quietly. Especially now." A pause. Under the door, I could see shadows of movement. "We just want to talk, Cullen. So you can make this easy, or you can make it hard. Up to you."

I gnawed on the inside of my cheek, then looked toward the bedroom. I closed the door tight and sucked in a breath. I would not let those assholes take one step closer to Grace and Ella, if I had to lie down and die to stop them. "I'll come outside."

I edged to the door, looking through the peephole to see the already nasty, unshaven face of Bruiser, his ruddy, puffy, scarred mug distorted even more through the fisheye glass. There were two other guys there I didn't know, young fresh faces, probably new recruits. Biding my time, I slowly pulled off the chain and unlocked the door.

Before I could pull it open, they barged in, slamming into my forehead, and the men tried to grab me. I skirted away before they could get a hand on me.

"Stay right there, fuckers," I said, poking the barrel of the gun into Bruiser's fat face. I grinned as they backed up, holding their hands up in surrender. I knew they'd try some shit like this. "Back the fuck up."

CULLEN

They started to, each of them grinning like this was fun for them. "Easy," Bruiser said. "Like I told you, we just want to talk."

"And I'm not really in the mood. Not after today. In fact, the last thing I want to do is talk to you assholes."

Bruiser smiled, baring yellow teeth. "Aw. That's not very friendly, Cullen."

"You know what's not very friendly? A fucking bomb," I snapped. "You're lucky I don't blow your fucking head off right now."

He shook his head and tsked at me. "We needed to show you that what happened at the office park will not be forgotten. You took out five of our men."

"Noted. Now get the fuck out of here."

He smirked at his two new guys, like *can you believe this shit?* They'd clearly already been brainwashed with the Fury Kool-Aid. "Maybe if you'd given us what we asked for, we wouldn't have had to resort to drastic measures."

"For the last time," I growled, "our business doesn't belong to you, and we're not giving it up."

Bruiser stared at me, fists clenched, his face turning even more scarlet.

"I've had enough of this walk down memory lane." I motioned to his two dumb bodyguards. "I'll give you ten seconds to tell me what this is about, or else you better leave me alone. You two, get the hell out."

Bruiser stared me down for a long while before nodding at them.

They turned to leave.

I looked at Bruiser as they retreated, closing the door behind them. He stared down the barrel of my gun, pointed right at his ruddy, asshole face, my trigger finger getting itchy as I thought of the shit they'd pulled earlier that day.

I wasn't sure I could wait ten seconds.

"So? I'm listening. Talk."

CULLEN

Chapter Twenty-Four

Grace

Ella stirred in my arms, but thankfully, did not wake up. I hugged her to my chest, patting her back. The last thing I needed was her making any noise now.

It was warming up in the closet, and Ella sweat a lot when she slept. When the air conditioner at the shelter was broken, she'd barely slept, and her little body was always moist with sweat, always red from the heat. I couldn't see much of her in the dark closet, but I could imagine her little mouth seeking out her thumb as she slept. I prayed that the motorcycles I'd heard outside the resort didn't belong to the Fury.

I peeked through the slats of the door. From here, I could just about see a small sliver of the enormous living area. Suddenly I heard a faraway banging on the door, and yelling. And then I saw Cullen reach in and close the door.

Oh, God. They're here.

I pulled Ella's onesie-dressed body to me. Her skin was clammy with sweat. I pushed to my knees and craned my head forward, trying to listen. I heard Cullen yelling. He didn't sound alarmed. In fact, his voice was just as in control as always. I couldn't make out a word of it.

I dared to believe that it was housekeeping, delivering towels. But I knew that was wrong. It was after two. And I knew for sure that Cullen wouldn't waste the breath or time yelling unless this was the Fury.

Then I heard a door slam, and the sounds of a scuffle in the living area. I shivered, expecting to hear at any moment the gunshot. Someone shouted, and it didn't sound like Cullen. Then a door slammed closed. I peeked again, hoping to see something, but the door was still closed.

I hoped to God that was the end of it. But then I heard another voice. Inside the living room, now.

Ella was now drenched, in my arms and getting hot. I grabbed a pillow with one hand and laid it down

CULLEN

on the floor, then eased her onto it, hoping she'd be more comfortable without my body heat. Then I leaned closer, until my ear was against the sliding door, and I could just make out the voices.

I swallowed as the man let out a long, low laugh, as if Cullen had just said the most hysterical thing ever. It sent a chill down my spine.

I signed up for this, I thought, holding Ella by the toe. I had the chance to escape this shit, and I didn't.

I really hoped, as I heard Ella squirm on the pillow, that I hadn't made a mistake.

I hadn't been raised on religion, but I needed all the help I could get. Pushing sweat-soaked hair from my face, I closed my eyes, brought my hands together, and prayed to the Big Man upstairs.

EVIE MONROE

Chapter Twenty-Five

Cullen

The last thing I wanted to do in the middle of the fucking night was sit around at the massive dining table in the Warner bungalow of the Vanderbilt, kicking back drinks with fucking Bruiser from Hell's Fury.

But I didn't have any choice.

My phone buzzed in my pocket, but I couldn't look at it. Again and again, it buzzed. It'd probably be another good twenty minutes before Hart and the rest of the guys arrived. If my message was good enough and they even came at all.

Bruiser pulled open the door on the minibar and took out a can of Heineken. Popping the top, he sucked down a gulp and wiped his mouth with the back of a leather, fingerless-gloved hand. Then he grabbed a bag of chips and poured half of the contents down his throat. A lot of it stuck on his goatee, the gross piece of shit.

EVIE MONROE

I didn't lower the gun.

"You really know how to live it up, boy," he said, striding toward the doors to the balcony and looking out. He stopped right in front of the bedroom door. "These are some fine digs."

"Yeah. Well. It'd be finer without your ugly ass here," I muttered.

He chuckled. He looked around the room as he drank, his eyes catching on the closed door to the bedroom. The crib shoved against the far wall must've escaped his attention. Maybe the crass asshole thought all fancy hotel digs came with a baby bed in the living room. He didn't say a word, but I knew what he was thinking.

"So?" I muttered. "Talk."

"Not until you lower your gun." He leaned over and grabbed a Miller Lite from the bar, sat down and slid it across the table. There were still chips in his beard. "You look like you could use this."

CULLEN

I didn't take my hand off the trigger. Didn't even look at the beer. I sat down at the head of the glass table and put my feet up on it, all the while keeping the gun steady. "I'm good. But let's get this over with. I've got things to do."

He laughed, pointing toward the bedroom, where Grace was huddled, scared out of her mind. "You have a *bitch* to do, is that right? Heard she was mighty hot. Cute little strawberry blonde with the nice tits? We've got a slew of guys here at the Fury who'd line up for a taste of that."

Fuck. Of course they'd been keeping tabs on her.

"She give good head? Deep throat that legendary Cullen McKnight cock all the ladies talk about? I bet she does, considering how all the rumors say your ass is whipped. Never thought I'd see the day. That true?"

I ignored him. "Say what you came to say or get the fuck out."

"Hearts all over the Bay are breaking, boy. Why don't you bring your sweet little piece out here and ask her if she'll have you for good, knowing what all us Fury know?" He leaned forward. "That you're nothing but a little pussy who was neglected by his rock star daddy and who's always been afraid he's not good enough?"

A fire that this douche had lit the moment he came in here suddenly started to blaze out of control in my veins. I pressed my finger on the trigger. He had no idea how close he was to a hole in the head.

He crushed the empty beer can in his fist and set it down. "You're not very hospitable, there, McKnight. Anyone ever tell you that?" When I didn't answer, he leaned against the door. "All right. I'll get right down to it. That message we sent was just the beginning. We want you gone. All Cobras, gone from Aveline Bay. It's Fury territory now."

That ripped a chuckle from me. "Really? And . . . why couldn't Slade tell me that in person? Is he too busy? Or too pussy?"

"He's got other fish to fry," he said, dismissive. Like there was anyone else bigger in this town than me. The guy was just a pussy. Pure and simple. "But he'd tell you the same thing. We want you gone. Do you understand?"

"Yeah, I understand. You're Slade's little whipping boy. And Slade can't fight his own battles, so what does that make you?" I fixed him with a sly smile and leaned back in my chair. "But I have two words in reply, and you can tell your boss they came straight from me: Fuck you."

Bruiser's smile faded.

"The Cobras have been in Aveline Bay way before the Fury ever came to town. It's our territory. We're not going anywhere. Fury doesn't scare us. And I'm sure as hell not going to take orders from a lackey."

His face tightened. He looked down at the ground.

"Well," he said, letting out a heavy sigh. "That's a shame. That's a real shame. Slade ain't gonna like to hear that."

I laughed. "Too fucking bad. Tell him if he's ever interested in coming to me and talking Prez to Prez, he might have a better chance. Otherwise, I don't want any of you assholes to waste my time. You're not worth it."

He shrugged and dug his hands into the pockets of his jeans. "I guess it is too bad, Cullen. I'll let him know."

So that was it. Suddenly I was eager to get out of there. Get out and take Grace and Ella far away. The second they left, that's what we would do. Go someplace else. Someplace safe.

He made like he was going to leave, and I relaxed for a split second.

Big fucking mistake.

He faked me out, turned right while heading left. For a fat guy, he was fast. He grabbed the handle of the bedroom door and busted in before I could take aim. I got off a single shot, the bullet burying itself in the wall as he disappeared from view.

"Shit!" I breathed as I heard the closet door open. I threw my feet off the table, jumping up and barreling into the room. "Bruiser, don't you—"

CULLEN

I froze in the doorway, the rest of the words caught in my mouth. I was too fucking late.

Bruiser was holding Grace in front of him like a shield, his arm wrapped around her neck. She was sobbing, tears falling down her cheeks, and shaking as he dragged her up against his fat greasy body.

The barrel of his gun was pressed firmly against Grace's temple.

EVIE MONROE

CULLEN

Chapter Twenty-Six

Grace

I'd been leaning with my ear against the door, trying to hear the murmurs from the other room, when suddenly the door exploded open. I screamed as a gunshot went off. I looked out the door to see a large man in a Hell's Fury *kutte* scanning the room. I pressed myself against the back wall of the closet and drew my knees into my chest, but a second later, the door flew open.

Ella started to wail at once as a hand reached in and grabbed a handful of my hair, yanking me out on my knees. He pulled me to my feet and I felt something cold push against the side of my head.

A gun.

Cullen burst through the open door a blink later, gun drawn. His voice was firm. "Let her go, Bruiser."

The Fury member pulled me closer in response. "Look at this tasty bitch!" he squealed. "Woo, Cullen, boy. You've outdone yourself with this one. You know what, they're right. She's got some nice tits. I bet she does give good head."

Cullen's voice was even and hard. "Let. Her. Go. I won't ask again."

I could tell by the way he laughed, as I felt his enormous belly jiggle against my back, that Cullen had some history with this disgusting person. He smelled of body odor and beer, and his beard scratched the side of my face. He wasn't going to let me go that easily.

"You know, Cullen. I don't think so. You had the chance to leave quietly. I think we're beyond that. And I think it's time we bit the head off of this Cobra. Your little pussy boys will be lost without you. They'll probably run screaming for the hills."

Cullen's arm stiffened as he readjusted his finger on the trigger and his eyes locked on mine. He was clearly not listening to this man's taunts. Sweat trickled down his forehead. "I'm warning you. She has nothing to do with any of this. If you don't want to be sucking on the barrel of my gun, you'd . . ."

CULLEN

"NO," Bruiser warned, his voice shaking the walls. "You'd better. You'd better shut your hole and listen for once, Mr. President, Mr. High and Mighty. Now, get down on your fuckin' knees."

Ella was starting to wail louder, and I shook, knowing I couldn't go to her. I hoped Cullen knew what he was doing. I trusted him, but for the first time, as his gaze locked on mine, I saw the cracks in his façade. "Like hell I will."

But the cracks only seemed to widen when Bruiser heard the crying too and drew me back toward the closet. "This your kid, Cullen? Is Cullen a baby daddy?"

He ripped at my hair to get me to shut up. I let out a shriek as pain screamed down my scalp, to the nape of my neck. More tears squeezed out of my eyes.

"Don't touch her," Cullen seethed, veins popping up in his hands, his arms, his neck.

"Aw, you make such a sweet family. Mom, baby, and little pussy McKnight." I felt his head swinging toward the closet, toward Ella, and my heart ached with the need to protect her. "Why don't we ask her, since we're all here together?"

He nuzzled his face into the side of my hair and sniffed. "Mmmm. She smells good. So, sweetness, what do you think? You think this pussy piece of shit Cullen is your happily ever after?"

He poked me to respond, but I stifled a whimper in return, and shoved at him. Cullen was more of a man than any Fury would ever be.

Cullen moved deeper into the room, his jaw working, and I could tell he was thinking. All the while he kept the gun out, narrowing his eyes to aim in Bruiser's direction. Was he trying to get off a shot? Did he think he could kill Bruiser, even with me as his shield? That was a big chance.

A chance I knew Cullen wouldn't take unless he was absolutely sure he could pull it off. He wouldn't risk my life. I was trembling, my heart was beating a mile a minute, but I willed myself to be absolutely still and not make this any more difficult for him than it already was.

CULLEN

Suddenly, I heard the door out front fly open. For a split second I dared to hope it was our salvation, maybe the other Cobras here to help, but then two more Fury arrived, guns drawn. They took in the scene, then pointed their weapons at Cullen as he took a step toward the wall, never lowering his gun.

Had Cullen even called for help? I wasn't even sure. I wouldn't put it past him to think he could handle everything on his own.

Cullen sucked in a breath as his eyes scanned them. I stifled a sob. I couldn't stand it if Cullen gave up now. I was only able to fight because he was.

"Hey. Take me instead," he said suddenly. "Let's stop playing around. You don't want her, you want me. Let her go and I'll drop my gun. Okay?"

Bruiser laughed. "We don't want to take you anywhere, boy. We have no need for prisoners. Especially you. You got that?"

The other men laughed sadistically. One of them sneered, "Yeah, man. Chop the head off the snake."

A low rumble emanated from deep within his chest, almost like thunder. He nodded. "Okay, fine. But just let her go and promise you won't hurt her. I don't give a shit what happens to me."

I could barely breathe. Ella screamed in the background, but what I heard louder than anything, was my own beating heart. My brain buzzed as blood shot hot and urgent through my veins. Sweat poured down my ribcage. It occurred to me just what Bruiser was saying. My life, in exchange for his.

Cullen was going to die. For me.

"No," I murmured, shaking my head. "No. Please."

"Get on your knees, asshole," Bruiser said. "And drop your fucking piece."

No. He couldn't do that. Cullen, unarmed, against these three, could never be a good thing. He was walking into certain death, for me. "Cullen," I wailed. "Don't."

CULLEN

"Hey," he said to me gently, his eyes softening. "It's all right."

"I love you," I blurted, wanting desperately to touch him. To hold him. To feel his arms around me, just one last time. That time in the hot tub, and on the bed, only a few hours ago? So much bliss . . . and now it was over. How could the best and worst night of my life be one in the same? Tears clouded my vision, but I blinked them away in desperate effort to see him. "Please. Cullen, I love you."

"I know you do, baby," he said, as easy and relaxed as always, as if he was resigned to this fate. "Don't worry."

Gaze fixed on mine, Cullen's lips moved, but I couldn't make out what he was saying. It felt like a secret message, just for me. I wanted desperately to understand, wondered if I would *ever* know, but a second later, his eyes went back to Bruiser, where they stayed, turning dark and cold.

Shoulders tense, arms wavering in front of him as he held the gun, his eyes twitched. He wiped sweat out of his eyes with his forearm. I could tell he was done. That even if he wasn't ready, he didn't have a choice. He took a deep breath, exhaling slowly.

"We're waiting, McKnight." Bruiser grinned sickly, his foul breath making me want to puke, and I could tell that this was something he'd been waiting a long time to see.

Cullen McKnight, President of the Steel Cobras. The father of my baby and the only man I'd ever loved. Humiliated. Dead.

I shuddered, stomping my feet, trying to tear myself loose from Bruiser's big hands. These assholes wanted me to witness Cullen's downfall, but I couldn't bear to see this.

His chest slick with sweat, his muscles tense, Cullen ran his tongue over his lips. He loosened his grip on the gun.

And he slowly dropped to his knees.

Chapter Twenty-Seven

Cullen

On my knees, I had the gun dangle on my finger before letting it fall to the carpet. My eyes scanned to my boots, on the other side of the room. I didn't have either of my weapons now.

Bruiser laughed. Long and hard. The asshole had been waiting for this day for a long time.

"Okay. Let her go," I growled. Grace was still in his arms, still trembling, eyes closed, her lips moving in a silent prayer.

He gave me a dismissive wave. "In a minute. Hands behind your head."

He was milking this, now, on a power trip. I did as he said, giving him a defiant look. "Now. Let her go, fucker."

Bruiser shook his head and sauntered over to me, still holding the gun to Grace's temple. "Let me enjoy this a little."

That was not a good sign.

Grinning down at me, he suddenly spat at me, foul-smelling saliva spraying my face. I refused to blink, to let him have that satisfaction. He motioned to the other guys, who came over and did it as well, hocking up saliva in their throats over and over again, until it was dripping from my chin, running down my neck, thick and wet. The other guys got off on it, too, making a show of it, seeing who had the best aim.

All the while, I stared at them, my blood hot and raging in my veins, wanting to rip their fucking heads off.

Only one thing went through my mind, as far as they were concerned. If I got out of this.

No.

Fucking.

Mercy.

CULLEN

"Let. Her. Go!" I repeated, the strength of my voice growing to a boom. "Now. Let her and the baby out of here right now. That was our deal."

He laughed. "You didn't say please."

He shoved Grace over to his two goons, who grabbed her, putting their hands all over her. One of them put his hands up her camisole, cupping her tits, and she whimpered. Now it'd gone too far. If I ever got out of here, I knew I'd kill them all, in the bloodiest way possible. No more making peace. I wouldn't rest until all of them were ripped limb from limb.

He came up close to me, running the gun through my hair, as if trying to style it. He leaned over and squeezed on my cheek. Patted my face. He was loving this, getting the best of a club president, since he'd never had the balls or the popularity to be one himself. The two goons behind him laughed, spurring him on. "I wonder what your guys would say if they could see King Cobra now, huh?" he asked them. He looked over at Grace. "What do you think, seeing your pussy-assed man like this? Not so badass, is he?"

But I wouldn't look at her. I could hear her whimpering. Feel her trembling. It was too much to know I'd brought this all on her. That I'd fucked her, just the way all those men had fucked over her mom. Just the way she knew I'd end up fucking her.

I flinched and scowled up at him. "You're going to get yours. Soon. And I'm going to fucking dance on your grave."

He brought his gun to my forehead, pushed the cold steel hard into the very center of my head, between my eyes. "Don't think so, Cullen, my boy. This is where you end."

As he cocked the gun, I managed a tight smile.

"I'll see you in hell," I hissed.

"You might," he grinned, pressing the gun harder into my skin. "But even then, you're never going to know what we did with your sweet little tasty bitch. We'll leave you to burn, wondering. But I'm telling you, it won't be pretty."

CULLEN

Fucking hell. They really weren't going to let her go after I was gone. No fucking wonder Nix had such a thirst for blood where the Fury were concerned. He was level-headed otherwise, but had no mercy for the Fury, because they'd done this to his girl, Olivia, too. They would have killed her, too, if we hadn't intervened. And I hadn't listened. I'd fought him on retaliation until the last possible moment. I'd been too soft. Tried to play nice, for the sake of my own stupidity.

Right then, I swore, as long as I lived, I'd never make that mistake again.

Bruiser's finger tightened on the trigger, and I knew it wouldn't be long.

But then, his smile dissolved, and I looked past the gun pointing between my eyes, catching him listening. I strained to hear over the sound of my pulse, pounding through my temples. Motorcycles. Fury . . . Or Cobras? The other men heard it, too, because one of them went into the living room. "I didn't think any of the other guys were. . ." he was mumbling as he stepped out.

EVIE MONROE

I knew the disruption was my best and last chance.

While Bruiser was distracted by the sound, I swung my arm out, pushing the gun's barrel off of my forehead. Stunned, Bruiser turned back and fired off a round, and the ceramic lamp at the night stand exploded. I rolled to the floor behind the bed, reached for my boot, grabbed my other piece, and fired off a single shot aimed at Bruiser's head.

The bullet caught him in his forehead and shaved off the top of his skull, showering me with blood and brain matter and bone fragments. I wiped the gore from my face in time to see him collapse to the floor in a heap, a stunned look on his face, like he didn't know what hit him.

I turned my gun to the other guy. Grace screamed in the man's grip, fighting against him. I heard the man shout, "You bitch," as I watched her lift her mouth from his arm, leaving a bloody half-circle-shaped bite mark on his forearm. She'd fucking bit him, tearing off a chunk of his skin. A woman possessed, her hair flying in her face, she kicked backwards, yanking violently.

Fuck! Where did this Grace come from?

The guy was no match for her. He tried to turn his gun to her as she let out a shriek, all flailing arms and legs, elbowing it out of his grip before he could aim. When she saw me, she wrenched herself free from him and ducked, flattening herself on the ground.

I fired off a shot, hitting him in the chest, and he staggered backwards, clutching his heart, falling in front of the bathroom door.

"Cullen!" she screamed.

Reaching for her and shoving her aside, blocking her with my body, I quickly turned to the other guy, who was just returning from the living room, his gun drawn. He put his hands up, dropping his weapon. "Hey. Wait."

"I don't wait," I muttered, still pumped with adrenaline after what they'd done to Grace.

Fuck that. I wasn't going to wait again. Didn't care that he was new Fury blood. He'd picked the wrong goddamn side.

I fired off two rounds into his head. He sunk to his knees, a small river of blood trickling into his eyes, before falling face-first to the ground.

Grace slunk down onto the bed, breathing hard, vising her head in her hands. Her wide eyes scanned the dead bodies at her feet. "Oh. Oh my God. Oh my God."

I went to her, knelt down in front of her. "You okay?" I couldn't touch her; I was full of spit and gore.

It didn't matter to her. She wasn't looking at me. Still shaking, she pushed away from me, and crawled toward the closet. It was only then that I heard Ella's crying. Grace came out of the closet, gathering Ella to her chest, shushing her softly. By the time I crawled over there, Ella had calmed and was cooing softly, smiling up at her mother's face.

CULLEN

Fierce. Caring. Loyal. Grace was born to be a mother. Born to be the mother of my kids. And with a woman this good in Ella's life, I figured I couldn't fuck things up too much. I'd give it my best shot.

I crawled up and staggered to the bathroom and ran my head under the shower to clean the Fury shit off my head and my face. I could hear Grace escape to the living room as I grabbed a towel, wiping myself clean, dry, stepping over the carnage as I joined her in the living room.

I leaned over and kissed them both, ready for whatever came next.

EVIE MONROE

CULLEN

Chapter Twenty-Eight

Grace

Stunned.

Shaking.

Scared to fucking death.

I cradled Ella in my arms, clinging to her, needing her and her sweetness as much as she needed my arms around her, comforting her. I needed to get everything I'd seen out of my head.

But I didn't think that was possible. Seconds had passed, and I already knew these memories would be seared in my brain forever.

The bleeding bodies were still scattered around us. These men's lives had just ended. Cullen had just taken them down in a shootout, right in front of me, without a second thought. He'd done it like he did everything else, with precise, almost clinical calmness.

EVIE MONROE

I held Ella to my chest as I sensed a warm presence behind me. At first, I flinched, but then I settled into it, knowing it was the man who'd promised to protect me, no matter what. It was uniquely Cullen, whose arms I fit into better than anyone else's. Who, even after all this, made me feel like I was home.

"Hey," he whispered into my ear. "You all right?"

I couldn't bring myself to answer. Because no, I was far from all right. I was getting better though, nestled in his arms. I just wanted him to hold me in this quiet cocoon a little while longer.

"Ella all right?" He ran a hand through her curls and she cooed happily. My chest swelled with relief.

I hugged him back, tighter, wrapping my hand around his neck. His skin was damp; I breathed in the sweet scent of his sweat, a scent that felt like home. "I can't believe you did that."

"I told you," he said, nonchalant, though even I could feel his heart beating double-time in his chest. "I'm never gonna let anything happen to you or Ella."

CULLEN

Holding tight to me, he lifted me to my feet, and, shielding my eyes from the bodies on the floor in the next room, walked me through the living room, and out the open front door.

Outside, on the tree-lined path, crickets chirped on, undaunted by what had happened here. Sirens wailed in the distance. I kept my head down, my face buried in his chest, Ella pressed against my breast as I heard the sound of someone running and faraway chatter. On the path ahead, a voice shouted, "Cullen! What the fuck happened?"

I looked up to see one of the men who'd been outside the warehouse coming toward us, gun drawn.

"They're dead, Hart. Bruiser too," Cullen said, voice hard, pointing the way behind us. "I had to leave our stuff."

"Bruiser? Shit." He gnashed his teeth. "What the hell? He came after you?"

"I'll call church later," Cullen said, guiding me toward the parking lot. "I've got to get these two away from here. Get in there and clean up as much as you can, get the stuff we left, then get your ass out of there. The police'll be here any second."

More people were running now, gathering on the path outside the bungalows, wondering what the hell was going on. They were murmuring that they'd heard the gunshots. More guys in Cobras *kuttes* arrived, too, but Cullen silently signaled to them to turn around and go back. He had a hundred-dollar bill out before he got to the valet. "Hey," he said to the teenaged boy at the stand. "Be quick about it, okay?"

The kid's eyes scanned over us. We were both barefoot, and Cullen was only wearing jeans, his gun sticking out from the waistband. I was still trembling. The boy opened his mouth to speak but Cullen shut him down. "NO questions."

The kid nodded and ran off.

He returned with the car a moment later, opening the door for me. As he did, I saw the flashing red and blue lights of the police cruisers. There wasn't time to get Ella into her seat, so I put her on my lap. Cullen

CULLEN

slammed the door, slid over the hood to the driver's side, got in, and gunned the gas. We tore out of the lot as the police were arriving.

"What about your guys?" I asked, looking over my shoulder as one, three, five police cars pulled in, choking the roundabout. This place was about to become a circus.

His hands loosened on the steering wheel as we pulled onto the highway. "Them?" He shook his head. "If anyone knows how to deal with the cops, it's my guys. They'll be fine. Are *you* okay?"

That question again. I nodded, but I wasn't sure. I was better than the last time he'd asked. My heart was still pounding out of my chest. My head hurt. I couldn't stop thinking of how those men looked as they died. How I'd been so close to losing Cullen. I opened my mouth to say I was, but instead, a sob slipped out.

"Hey." He reached over and put a hand on the back of my neck, his big, callused fingers caressing me with uncharacteristic softness. He pulled over to the side of the road. "We'll be okay."

I nodded. "I know. I just can't stop thinking."

Ella started to squirm. He got out of the car and lifted her out of my arms. He placed her in the car seat in the back.

In the darkness, I heard a little, sleepy voice say, "Daddy, hold me."

I whirled. "Did she just ask you to . . .?"

He let out a short laugh. "Yeah."

I smiled, until I was hit with a stabbing realization. She'd been so close to losing her Daddy tonight. I shuddered.

When we took off again, he kept his hand in mine, on my knee, his fingers slowly stroking my thigh. I was exhausted. Scared. Didn't know if I wanted to laugh or cry. All the while, he kept repeating that we would be okay.

When we pulled up at his house, I blinked. I didn't think I'd ever see this place again. And this was Aveline Bay. Where the Fury lived. Bruiser said we weren't welcome here. They wanted the Cobras—and Cullen

CULLEN

especially—out. Bruiser might have been dead, but there were others. I looked up at the massive white mansion and started to shiver uncontrollably.

"I told you, I'm not going to let anything happen to you," Cullen said.

"But what you did . . .those guys . . ." I babbled.

He nodded, my fears were real. "Right. But I'll keep you safe, Grace. I promise you, I will." He motioned to the door. "Let's go on in so you can get some rest."

I got out, trembling, as he reached into the back and pulled out a sleeping Ella. We went inside, where he laid Ella on her bed, covered with her favorite pink sheets again. I watched him, lingering in the hallway, thinking of that man Bruiser's hands on me, his gun pressed up against my temple. I shuddered to think what could have happened. I could still smell his stench on me. It didn't matter how many times I told myself I was safe. I kept looking around, expecting to see him crawling out of the shadows.

When Cullen turned back to me and saw the look on my face, he put a finger under my chin and gently tilted my face up. He kissed my lips. "Hot bath?"

I sighed with relief at the thought. "Yes."

He opened up the double doors to his extravagant master bath, with the huge corner tub, in front of a giant curved picture window that offered a 180-degree view of the Pacific Ocean. It was dark, but there were a few ships silently slipping by, their lights blinking in the distance.

He knelt in front and started to run the water for me. I stood in the door, blankly watching the water fill the tub as he swirled his hand in it to check on the temperature. "Take off your clothes."

I looked down. My clothes were splattered with blood. I cringed and started to panic. I couldn't do this. No matter how much I loved him.

He cupped my cheeks in both hands, kissed my forehead, and said, "I know you're afraid. You've been through a lot tonight. I just want you to know I will keep you and Ella safe. The bad guys are gone."

"Yeah, but for how long? Cullen, I . . ." When I looked up at him, I saw he still had that man's spit on his shirt.

"Baby. Let's take a hot bath and relax a little. It's late. We're both exhausted. I promise. You're safe now. Let me help you out of these clothes."

I smiled. He sure seemed eager. I pointed to the picture window. "Will the neighbors be able to see me? Barry has a heart condition, you know."

"Yeah? I'll make sure I parade around outside naked more often," he said.

I looked up at him, my face too tired to make a scowl.

"Kidding." Releasing me, he pressed a button on the wall that made some blinds slide closed, then motioned me forward to an electric panel beside the tub. He started to explain what all the controls did—

dimming the lights, changing the speed of the jets, adjusting the temperature.

I stared at it, only half listening. I wouldn't use any of those. I just wanted to sink into the tub and relax. But most of all, I wanted to forget. Forget everything I'd seen. And felt.

He adjusted the lighting, turning off most of the lights except for two sconces, which glowed with an almost-real looking orange flicker of candlelight. It was so pretty. Relaxing. Romantic. Normal. I could get used to this. "Good?" he asked.

I nodded numbly.

"Want music?" He pointed to a button on the console.

"Um, okay."

"What's your poison?" He thought for a moment. "Lemme guess. Nineties pop?"

I nodded sheepishly, a little amazed he still remembered what he'd once called my awful taste in music. He'd always been into Led Zeppelin, Pink Floyd and classic rock.

He turned a dial to a channel called 90's on 9 from Sirius Satellite Radio and immediately, Billy Idol's Cradle of Love came on. This would do. I nodded.

He rolled his eyes to the ceiling, grabbed a bunch of towels from a shelf and handed them to me. "Take your time. Stay in as long as you want. Let me know if you want anything."

Right then, I didn't need the big tub, or the pretty view, or all the bubbles. I wanted him. I imagined myself, sliding in across from him, into the bubbles, resting my bare feet on his big, broad chest as he stroked my legs under the water, his callused fingers walking their way up my body. That sounded like heaven.

Maybe that could make me believe in normal.

But we'd been through so much. He was tired. He may have looked like he had it all together, but he'd just killed three men. He couldn't simply forget that, could he? He may have talked a good game, but I refused to believe he was so hardened as to think killing people was a normal occurrence. No, he'd had to have felt that, in a deep place he never talked about. I bet he just wanted this day to end.

I nodded. "Thanks."

When he left, closing the doors behind him, I pulled off my clothes, thinking I'd have to burn them. I never wanted to wear them again. I turned to look at myself in the mirror. True to his name, Bruiser had given me bruises. Red welts were starting to pop out on my shoulders and neck, where he'd grabbed me. I leaned forward and traced the spot on my temple, where the gun had been. It was tender to the touch.

I reached my toe into the frothing water. Perfect temperature. The tub was huge. I almost wished it was smaller. I hadn't had a bath since I was a kid. I turned off the water, stepped inside the tub, and made myself comfortable. I immersed myself in the water, found soap, lathered, and washed. I dunked my head,

CULLEN

shampooed, and rinsed until the water was covered with a film of suds.

Then I rested my head against the sloped side of the tub.

But I couldn't close my eyes.

Whenever I did, I saw Cullen kneeling there, with his hands behind his back, a hopeless position if ever there was one. I saw Bruiser, with the gun barrel pressed against his forehead, about to pull the trigger and end his life. We were so close to an outcome that would've destroyed everything I'd ever wanted.

So I cried. I sobbed and sobbed until I was all cried out. Until there was not a tear left in my body to shed. If things had gone differently, I'd have been all alone. Ella would've grown up without a daddy.

Suddenly, my blood ran cold. I sat up, shivering.

I didn't just want him there. I needed him there, with me, right now.

"Cullen!" I cried, sitting up straighter, hugging myself.

A moment later, he burst through the doors, wearing just his boxer briefs, a dazed, bleary look in his eyes, like he'd been sleeping. He probably *had* fallen asleep, considering Cullen could doze off in the drop of a hat. His eyes circled around the room, looking for the problem.

I held up the washcloth shyly. "Sorry to bother you. But I don't have anyone to do my back."

He let out a sigh of relief and extended his palm to me. "You asked the right person. Give it here."

He crouched down on the fluffy bathmat besides me, took the washcloth from me, and dipped it in the water.

He hooked a finger toward me. "Come closer."

I moved from the lip of the tub, closer to him. He leaned over and started to run the cloth slowly over my back. I sighed, leaning into his touch. "You're tense, baby. Relax."

I could feel the stiffness in my neck. Every part of me felt like it'd been wound tight. "How are you not?

CULLEN

How can you just fall asleep after what we've been through? I don't think I'm going to fall asleep ever again."

He shrugged and yawned. "I'm fucking tired."

"You're filthy, too. But those men. They could've killed you. And you killed them."

He didn't say anything for a long time. He just slowly worked the washcloth over my back. "Yeah." He studied me for a little while. "Hell, Grace. I didn't want to. You know I didn't want to. But I couldn't let them walk all over the Cobras. I don't like that I had to do it. But I'd do it again in a second if it means I keep you safe."

"I know," I said, and I felt such a rush of love for him that I couldn't control myself. I reached for him, putting my hands on his bare chest. "You should come in here with me."

The corners of his lips twisted into a smile at my eagerness. "If you let me choose the music."

I didn't even know the song that was playing now. I figured giving up my music was a small price to pay. I nodded and he flipped the switch to the Classic Rock station. Immediately, Pink Floyd emanated from the speakers above.

My taste in music wasn't as bad as he thought. Actually, I secretly loved the song that was playing.

He stood up, slid off his briefs, while I watched, whatever fear I'd harbored slowly transforming to unbearable need. His body was all peaks and valleys, strong and tattooed and ripped. And that cock . . . it was masterful, a true work of art. How was it that every time I saw him, he only looked more beautiful?

I moved forward as he stepped in, sliding into the tub behind me. I settled my ass between his legs. Then he pulled me back against him, and I felt his lips silently forming the lyrics to the song. I nestled my shoulder blades against the strong planes of his chest, letting his furnace-like warmth seep into me. His cock throbbed against the small of my back, growing between us.

CULLEN

"You ever fucked in a bathtub?" he whispered into my wet hair as he wrapped his arms around my waist and hugged me close to him.

I shook my head and leaned my wet hair back against his broad chest, feeling like, yes, this was heaven. He grabbed the warm wet washcloth and scrubbed it across his face. The bubbles landing on his beard. God, what a beard. The man was pure sex. Pure, hot, agonizingly beautiful sex on a stick.

He ran his hands across my stomach, tickling me lightly, his fingers moving in time to the song. Then he dipped his head forward and licked at my neck.

"You're about to."

I let out a laugh. "What happened to just relaxing and taking it easy?"

"Later." He sucked my earlobe gently into his mouth and ran his tongue over it. I wriggled against him slightly, feeling his cock, now huge and rock-hard, against my back.

I turned my head, our gazes locking as I met his lips and kissed him softly. I pushed my tongue into his mouth, tangling with his, letting out a little moan. His body, so hard and ripped against mine, was perfect.

"Yeah, good plan," I said, when I tore my mouth from his. "We can definitely relax later."

I reached up with one hand and held his face while taking his tongue deeper, opening my mouth wider as the slick, wet sounds of our furious kissing filled the room. Under the water, I felt one hand slide down my tummy, brushing between my legs. He licked at my lips as he slowly inserted a finger inside me.

It was good. My forehead fell against his shoulder. "Cullen . . ." And just like that, I came a little.

The song ended. Another one came on, nothing I knew. Cullen did, though. I could tell from the way he moved in time to the beat.

His other hand slid up and cupped my breast, the pad of his thumb slowly stroking my nipple. I squirmed on him and lifted my mouth to his, kissing his stubble-covered jaw as he stroked inside me, carefully inserting another finger. He lifted his mouth from mine and began kissing my neck, licking down to my shoulder.

"What is this song?" I asked him.

He chuckled a little. "Queen. Don't Stop Me Now."

There was no way on Earth I was ever going to stop him. I tilted my pelvis, rocking on his hand, letting these sharp jolts of pleasure course through me with every stroke.

How the hell he did this to me, I'd never know. But one moment I was fine, just a little turned on, and the next I was ravenous. Like he flipped a switch, and suddenly I wasn't afraid, or worried, or even a little concerned. The fear went away, the need took over, and I couldn't think of anything but him, him, him.

He started to rub my clit as he pumped. I arched my back and my breasts thrust out of the water. His eyes darkened as he saw my nipples, hard and wet, glistening in the candlelight.

EVIE MONROE

I pulled away from his mouth and rolled over so that I lay on top of him. I slid my body up and felt his cock against my stomach. I smiled up at him and touched his face, feeling loved and wanted and precious to him. God, he was so sexy, watching me with those dark eyes in the candlelight.

Even if this wasn't normal, I was all-in.

I spread my legs over his and slid upward, placing my hands on either side of his stubble-covered cheeks as I kissed him gently on the lips. "I love you, Cullen."

His eyes locked on mine, and he said exactly what I expected: "Yeah. I know, baby."

When I rose up and straddled his thighs, he let out a groan. I could tell from the way he scraped his top teeth over his lower lip that this was what he was looking forward to. He licked his lips in anticipation. His eyes swept over my breasts, now out of the water, nipples bobbing on the surface, before catching and holding my gaze.

CULLEN

I reached down, under the water, and let my fingers glide over his hard cock. I wrapped my hand around the thick shaft and lifted it. He let out another breath of restless anticipation, resting his arms out on the ledge of the tub.

His cock twitched in my palm. It'd always been calm, unshakeable Cullen McKnight, so it was nice to get that little rise out of him. I lifted up onto my knees a bit, guiding his cock until it was under me. I moved slightly, adjusting, then found the right spot. I paused with him right at my entrance, as the song switched again, to something slower, now.

Taking a deep breath, with his gaze, heavy-lidded and full of adoration, urging me on, I slid the head of his cock inside me, feeling it pushing its way in. Trembling, I slid down and took him deep inside me, all at once. I felt him almost up to my heart. I placed my hands on his chest, feeling his heart beat as I leaned my forehead against his, gasping into his mouth.

"I love this," I said, almost laughing with how good it felt. "Being with you, like this."

He let out a rasp, catching my breath with his own, and his hands encircled my waist. "No place I'd rather be, baby."

Bracing my palms on his shoulders, I rose upward and let him slide almost all the way out, then slipped back down.

I adjusted, I squirmed, I rubbed myself shamelessly on his body, moving on his hard cock, finding the rhythm that made my body come alive. As tired as I was, I found my energy renewed by every guttural groan that was torn from his throat. "That's right. That's my good, bad girl," he said through clenched teeth. "Ride me."

I smiled against his mouth and repeated that perfect movement over and over, squeezing his cock inside me, hard, every time I crashed down onto him.

"Nice, baby girl. That's it." He ran his hands over my breasts, licking and kissing my lips. He slid his hands lower to my hips, urging me to go faster. He tangled his tongue with mine, stroking it into my mouth in time with my riding him. I felt his body twitching and I knew he was close. "Just like that. Grace, fuck . . . the things you do to me."

I cried out against his mouth and pumped faster, up and down over him, clenching him tight inside. I wrapped my arms around him, reached over and grabbed the side of the tub and cried out as the orgasm crashed through me.

He jutted his hips upward. Water splashed everywhere, falling to the floor as he grabbed my ass and thrust himself up into me. He groaned into my mouth and pumped in hard, straight to my center, coming apart inside me. I wrapped my arms around him and held onto him as he came, feeling his every shudder, fully prepared to never, ever let him go.

He fell back against the tub and cradled me against him, panting into my ear. I laid my head on his shoulder. He stroked his fingers up and down my back as we rested there, totally spent, the water cooling around us, not saying anything.

I slowly slipped out of him and laid myself down between his legs again, spent, but content.

He kissed the shell of my ear and twisted the faucet with his foot. "Need more water. I think we lost some."

"Oh, so we don't have to get out?"

"Hell, no. We don't have to do anything we don't want to do."

I smiled as I leaned against him. I liked that. I liked not doing the things that were expected of us. I liked being in control of our own destiny, for once.

"Oh, and baby?" he said, his fingers lightly tickling my abdomen, squeezing my nipples.

"Hmmm," I murmured, grinning, feeling absolutely fulfilled and very, very wanted.

I could feel his smile more than I could see it. He nestled up to my face, kissing the shell of my ear. "I love you, too."

And dammit, just when I was feeling like I'd been all cried out? He made me start to bawl again.

CULLEN

But this time, it was out of pure joy. It was all worth it. Everything. Every little fucked up thing that we'd been through. And everything to come. Because we were together, where we belonged.

Now, there was no doubt in my mind.

EVIE MONROE

Chapter Twenty-Nine

Cullen

The rest of the weekend went by in a blur. I spent two days home with Grace and Ella, cocooned in our home, making sure that they were recovered from what had happened over the weekend. As if they could recover. But we had to try.

On the third day, Grace walked into the kitchen as I was eating lunch, after she'd put Ella down for a nap. "Do you think it would be okay if I went next door with Ella sometime?"

I lowered the beer bottle I was drinking from and swallowed. "Why?"

She shrugged. "Barry stopped by while you were in the shower."

I frowned. "You opened the door?"

"Well, yes, Cullen," she said to me, rolling her eyes like she always did when I got overprotective. "I looked out the window. I saw her. It was fine."

"Yeah. But you shouldn't . . ."

"I can't even talk to *friends*?" she asked, flustered. "What are we, your tower princesses?"

I fought the urge to get angry. I knew this was going to happen. I couldn't keep her and Ella locked up inside for the rest of their lives. Eventually, they'd have to get out.

But I also knew that Slade was probably foaming at the mouth to get to me, in any way he could. Hart had learned from some online digging that the president of the Fury hadn't taken the loss of Bruiser and the other men well. Word on the street was that he was out for blood.

But other than that, there was nothing. No knowing when the Fury would strike. After being caught unaware with the bomb, I didn't want to make that mistake twice.

CULLEN

"No, you're not locked in, Grace, goddammit. But you know you have to be careful."

"I *am* being careful, Cullen," she said. "But Barry's granddaughter is over with her baby and she thought it would be a nice time for the girls to meet. They're at the age for playdates so it's normal. I can't stay in here forever. Ella can't."

I pinched the bridge of my nose, thinking. "Yeah. I know." I sucked in a breath. "So you'll just be in their backyard? When?"

She nodded. "Whenever you'll let me go."

I stood up and set my beer bottle in the sink. "Not today. I've got church."

Grace walked to the sink and put the bottle in the trash can under the sink.

"Okay, but I could—"

"You're not going without me," I said.

She looked surprised. "So, you're actually going to go next door? And be civil to our neighbors?

I shrugged. "Why not?"

She snorted. "This, I've got to see. I'm pretty sure Barry thinks you're an evil biker who's got me under his spell. She doesn't think there's any reason why we should be together."

I grinned. "Sweetheart, most people think that."

She nodded, agreeing with me. I sure as hell knew I wasn't the type of guy girls could bring home to mom.

"But I don't give a shit what any of them think," I said, coming up close to her and taking her chin in my hands. I kissed her lightly on the forehead as she wrapped her arms around my waist.

She grinned up at me. "How late are you going to be this time?"

"Just an hour. Two, tops."

She laughed. "I'm not holding my breath. We're eating dinner without you. And . . . probably going to sleep, too."

CULLEN

"Good plan." I looked around for my *kutte* and found it hanging in the closet in the room off the garage. It smelled fresh. The girl really did need to get out more. I slipped it on. "Where's my piece?"

She reached into one of the high cabinets over the refrigerator and pulled it out, closed up in a Ziploc bag, like Exhibit A, evidence of a crime. When I gave her a questioning look, she said, "I didn't want anyone getting to it."

"All right, but if it's hidden . . . *I* won't know where to find it when I need it. And what if I needed it?"

She pressed her lips together. "I guess. I just worry about having weapons in the house."

I guessed I'd have to get used to keeping my weapons in a safe place.

"We'll figure it out." I pinched her ass and she jumped, grinning, and swatted me. "See you."

I got into the Dodge Charger and drove down to Lucky's, keeping an eye out for anyone strange. I'd gotten at least a hundred messages since that night in

Santa Barbara, all of them from my guys, wanting to know what the hell was up. I'd responded to each one of them, telling them I'd call church in a few days. But time was running out. They were getting more and more restless. It felt like the Fury was taking that big breath, ready to come out with their guns blazing.

They had a big reason to, now.

And I may have been Public Enemy Number One, but they didn't just want me. They wanted the club. Every one of them had a target on his head.

Now the people we loved weren't safe, either.

When I got to Lucky's, there were a hell of a lot of bikes parked outside. I don't remember ever seeing so many. Hart was pulling one of the cars out of the bay, probably to make more room for the rest of the Cobras in the cramped space inside.

"Hey," he said. "You turning in the wheels?"

I hadn't had a chance to look into a new car for the family. We hadn't really talked about it but Grace had mentioned a minivan, which effectively shut me down.

CULLEN

No fucking way was I driving one of those. "Can I keep the Charger a little longer?"

"Knock yourself out. You get the stuff from Drake?"

I shook my head and gave him a fist bump. "I'll get it from him later. Thanks for doing that for me, man."

I'd been concentrating on Grace the rest of the weekend, and hadn't had time to go and pick up the suitcase, my boots, my gun, and the other things we'd left there when we split in a hurry. Drake had messaged me that night, telling me they'd taken care of everything, no problems. I'd had my hands full, trying to get Grace to feel a little sense of normalcy in the house with me.

"No problem. How's she doing?"

I looked at him. "She?"

"That's your girl, right? Her kid? Are they okay?"

"Yeah. They were shaken up. But they're better now."

I walked inside the open door, observing the tense faces of the men, all packed like sardines in the smoke-filled room. Hart closed the garage door for privacy.

"You gonna tell us what the fuck is up?" Jet asked, sulking, the hothead as usual.

Nix took a drag from his cigarette and punched his younger brother. He leaned in and said, "Hey man. Good to see you. There are a lot of rumors going around, so I think it's time you separated fact from fiction."

"Was just going to," I said, moving to the front of the room. I hopped up on the workbench and lit a cigarette. "Listen up. I'm sure you heard about the incident at the hotel in Santa Barbara over the weekend. I was there with my girl, and Bruiser and a couple other Fury showed up, wanting to talk. They told me that they wanted all Cobras to leave Aveline Bay for good. I told them under no circumstances was that gonna happen. Weapons were drawn, there was a fight, and I ended up taking all three of them out. I had no choice."

CULLEN

Zain said, "So it's true? You took out Bruiser?"

I nodded.

"So naturally Slade is gonna have it out for us. No question. But what he's up to now is anyone's guess."

I looked at Hart and he shrugged. "I haven't seen anything online."

"Why the fuck wasn't that pussy Slade there to deal with you on his own?" Jet asked. "They weren't at that party at their clubhouse, that's for sure."

"Yeah. It seems they were all expecting we'd go after them, so they staged that party so we'd end up with our thumbs up our asses. Then they sent their boys after me." I sucked on my cigarette and let out the smoke in a rush. "I'm sorry I couldn't be there for you guys. I wanted to be, but I have something I need to tell you all."

I looked over their faces. These are men who I'd promised they'd come first, ever since I assumed the reins as president. I knew I'd done the right thing, but it still felt like swallowing razor blades, admitting this.

"I was in Santa Barbara because I was protecting my girl, and my daughter. She's not quite two, and on Saturday, I was taking them out of town to keep them safe. That's where I got held up."

There was a moment of silence, where people traded glances. Finally, Hart said, "What the fuck?" I winced at that, until he said, "I feel like I'm in the Twilight Zone. Cullen's a daddy?"

Everyone laughed. "To a little girl, no less," he added. "Shit man, payback's a bitch."

They were all hysterical over that one. At first, yeah, it was awkward, but gradually, I relaxed into it. They weren't pissed about me missing the meeting. Hell, it was good to be a dad. To be a part of a real family, for the first time in my life. And I'd be damned if I'd ever tell anyone something that felt so right was wrong.

Nix came up to me, and fist bumped. "Congratulations man. What's her name?"

CULLEN

"Ella's my daughter," I said, taking out my phone and showing a picture I'd snapped earlier that day. "And Grace is my girl. They're living with me. And they need your protection."

The men nodded. Jet said, "You know you've got it. But we're not just going to hole up and defend ourselves against them, right? We're going to fight back?"

I nodded. "Fuck, yeah. As far as I'm concerned, we're at war. We're going to hit them, and hit them hard, and we're not going to stop until every last one of them is out of Aveline Bay. That's a promise."

Jet tightened his fists. "Yeah. Let's get 'em."

"I want all of you to have eyes in the back of your head. They're gonna be coming at us from all angles now and it's not gonna be pretty. If any of you need our protection, let us know. We have to watch out for each other, more than ever now. Got it?"

They all nodded.

"All right. So the officers and I are gonna go over some things over the next few days, try to get intel on the Fury's situation. The prospects are gonna have to be all in on this. No questions asked. If you hear of anyone has anything, needs anything," I held up my cell phone. "Doesn't matter how small. Text me and we'll be there, we'll check it out. We stick together in all this, and there is no way the Fury's gonna run us out of this town. Aveline Bay is Cobra territory. That ain't gonna change."

The men roared their approval, and for the first time, Jet actually didn't have anything snide to say. I figured that was progress as I snuffed out my cigarette and got ready to go back home.

Home. The mansion finally felt like a home.

"Hey," Nix said to me after most of the guys had left. "If we didn't have X's on our backs, I'd say we should all double date. You and Grace and me and Olivia."

CULLEN

I laughed. Double date. Did I ever think I'd hear Nix say those words to me? "Yeah. We'll take a raincheck on that one."

"So what did Bruiser say?" he asked.

"You know. He said Slade wouldn't rest until all Cobras were out of the bay. I told him no way in hell and thought I could reason with him, but then he went and grabbed Grace. At that point, I'd had it. He was dead. Started talking shit and threatening her and you know Bruiser. He was never that bright. So I took him out. Him and two new Furies. I don't know who they were. They must've followed the car over there."

"Fuck," Nix said. "Yeah, we've got to be careful. And you know we'll protect your girl. You call us, and we'll be there."

We walked out to the lot, where most of the bikes had already cleared out. He walked to his while I went to the Charger.

"You gonna get a new bike?" he asked me.

"Got one. My dad's." I took the picture out of my wallet and showed it to him.

He grimaced. "Indian, aye?"

I stared at the picture. My dad never wanted me touching the damn thing. Never rode it, either. It was all for show. But he was gone now. And that was my damn house, my things, my family. I was the man of my house, and I could do what I pleased. "Yeah. Figured I'd try it out. I'll probably go back to my Harley, though. Eventually."

He peeked inside the back of the car and grinned. "Car seat?"

"Fuck you." I grinned.

"Talk about a one-eighty. You're turning into a real family man," he said, slapping me on the back. "What the hell is this world coming to?"

I was going to tell him not to let anyone know, that it would crush my image, but fuck it. My dad had been all about image, wanting to be the fun party guy. And look where that got him.

CULLEN

Image was overrated. If any of these fuckers thought I wasn't capable of being president just because I had a family, then fuck them.

Still, I had to wonder. I crossed my arms and leaned against the Charger. "So, you had to have heard rumors. What were people saying? When the president of the Cobras didn't show up for his own meeting?"

Nix shrugged. "They were confused, at first. But they know you, man. They know how loyal you are. When you didn't show up, they knew you had to have a good reason."

I let out a breath of air. "I know she's a good enough reason to me."

A slow smile broke out on his face. "What are you wondering? Whether they're going to vote you out, man?" He smacked me on the shoulder. "Fuck that. You don't have to sell your soul to us, man. You can have a life. What you just said in there proves it. No one else could do what you do. I know I sure couldn't. We're damn lucky to have you."

EVIE MONROE

"Yeah. Thanks. See you man."

As I got in the car and gunned the engine, I let out a breath, then rolled down the window and let the cool breeze from the Pacific take me home.

Chapter Thirty

Grace

"Ugh, really, Ella?" I moaned as I turned away from the stove to catch her splashing jelly all over her new sundress. She'd been wearing a bib, but only God knew where that had gone.

As I rushed over to her, lifting the dress over her head as she laughed and shouted, "Really! Really! Really!"

I frowned. "Oh, you just think you're so cute, don't you?"

I took the sink and started scrubbing and the pink and white gingham check fabric with some dish soap when suddenly a heard a hissing sound from the stove. I turned in time to see the pot boiling over.

"Shit!" I shouted, dropping the dress in the suds in the sink and managing to push the pot off of the burner.

"Shit shit shit!" Ella cried.

"No! No! Don't say that." I semi-scolded her, wincing as I looked at the clock. We were due to be at the Sumter's in fifteen minutes for their family picnic. In a fit of insanity where I actually thought I could be Miss Happy Homemaker, I'd volunteered to bring a potato salad. Never mind that I'd never made potato salad, or anything potluck, in my life. Hell, I'd never even been to a potluck before. I'd gotten a recipe online, read the steps, and figured, how hard could it be?

But that was before Ella decided to keep me up all night with teething pain. Cullen had told me he'd handle it, but she screamed all night long, so even though he closed the door, I couldn't sleep. Then, when I started to work on the salad, I realized I'd forgotten . . . not some obscure ingredient on the list. No, I had all those. What I'd forgotten was . . . the damn potatoes.

Cullen had called church early, because there were rumors about the Fury flying around, and he

CULLEN

needed to stay on top of it all. So I'd had to call down to Whole Foods, and get the potatoes delivered. Then the washing machine had given out on me, flooding the entire laundry room, which was a joy to clean up.

Now, I was standing in the kitchen, in sopping clothes, unshowered, my hair like a bird's nest on the top of my head, ready to sob. I tried to pull myself together as I heard Cullen's motorcycle pulling up into the garage. I took a deep breath and wiped the tears from my eyes.

When he came in, I said, "Everything okay?"

He nodded, kissed me on the forehead, then went over and gave Ella a kiss. "You're not ready yet?" he asked me casually.

No shit, Sherlock. I clenched my fists and tried to keep it together.

He frowned when she smacked her sticky hands to his beard. "Shit shit shit!" she exclaimed.

He looked at me, a questionable smirk on his face.

Just as I started to sob.

Then he took Ella into his arms and said, "That ain't the way a good girl's supposed to talk." He started to walk upstairs. "Come on, baby. Let's get you upstairs to wash you up and give some mommy some alone-time."

I smiled gratefully at him as he went past me. As he did, he squeezed my ass again and murmured, "Take it easy, girl. They won't hang you if they don't have their potato salad."

I knew that. Barry had been nothing but sweet to me, especially in the past few weeks, since we'd come back from Santa Barbara. And knowing the way she entertained me like a regular Martha Stewart, my little potato salad was probably nothing compared to the spread she'd no doubt come up with. I'd go over there with Ella almost every afternoon, for snacks, and Ella and her granddaughter's little Tori, would play together on the swings as we sipped iced tea. It was so normal, so nice, exactly what I needed for Ella.

But I wanted to keep it going. I wanted to grow our relationship, so when Barry invited Cullen, me, and

CULLEN

Ella to a family get-together with all of the Sumter's friends and family from San Francisco, I jumped at the chance.

Later on, it hit me, how much was riding on this. Cullen still hadn't said so much as boo to either of the Sumter's. He was still closed-off, still rode down the street like a badass who'd run you over if you got in his way. Barry hadn't mentioned it, even though I kept peppering our talks with stories about the sweet things Cullen did for me.

That's why this potato salad had to be perfect. I didn't just want them to like me and Ella. I wanted them to like all of us. Love us. I wanted to make a potato salad of epic proportions.

Once the potatoes came, the rest of the potato salad wasn't hard to make. I was no cook, but I followed the recipe and tasted along the way, and I didn't think it'd give anyone food poisoning. I stuck it in the fridge and took the stairs two at a time, trying to get upstairs to get to the shower.

When I went in the bedroom, Cullen was standing in front of his dresser, half naked, trying to pick out a new shirt to wear. He lifted a white one out of the stack and looked at me. "You got it under control?"

I checked my phone and shook my head as I rushed for the shower, ripping my t-shirt over my head. "No, we should be there already. Where's Ella?"

"In her room. She's fine."

Great. As I undid my bra, still caught in the tangles of my shirt, I realized I'd left her dress in the sink. Fuck. "I've got to—"

I stopped as he clamped his hand over my wrist. I was still caught in the confines of my shirt as he pulled me toward him. I growled at him. I didn't need this now. He sat down on the bed, pushing the t-shirt down over my head so he could look me in the eye. "Hey. Look at me."

"I've got to . . ." I wriggled, but he held me firm. I eventually caved, because he was giving me that commanding Cobras president look that never failed.

CULLEN

"It's a party. No one will care if we're a half hour, hell, an hour late. Calm yourself, girl."

I was so worked up, my body shook. The tension spiraled off of me in hot waves.

"Deep breath."

I swallowed a gulp of air. Let it out, slowly. He was right. It did make me feel a little better. I stood there, between his open legs, as he looked up at me, hands clamped firmly onto both of my arms. Time was ticking.

"Now what?" I asked.

"Take another one."

I rolled my eyes. "I don't have time for this."

He gave me that silently commanding look.

I took another one. Felt a little better.

He reached up and lifted the shirt over my head. Pulled the undone bra straps from my shoulders, and off of my arms. He slowly wrapped a big, callused hand around my breast and brought the nipple to his mouth. He licked at it, and I was instantly wet.

"We can be a lot late, if you want," he said, wetting my nipple to a diamond-hard point. "I will not mind."

As good as it felt, I had too much riding on this. I shook my head. "Cullen. Please. I know you'd be happy if we never went to this thing at all. But it matters to me. A lot."

He kissed his way up my breastbone, up my throat, and to my chin. "Yeah. I know. I told you," he said, releasing me and tapping my ass toward the shower. "I'm down for it. Get ready."

I rushed into the shower and turned on the water, trying to take my time, like Cullen had said. But my nerves were completely shot. I imagined walking into a full backyard of strangers and having them look at us like we were lepers. I only managed a five-minute shower and shave before I felt like I was going to explode. I ran into the bedroom and started to dry my hair in front of the mirror, mentally going through my wardrobe to find my most conservative outfit. Hair still

CULLEN

wet, I tied it up in a ponytail and put on some quick mascara.

When I turned around, Cullen was holding my bright red, gauzy boho dress in front of me. "I can't wear that," I told him.

"Hell, yes, you can. You look hot in it."

"But I don't want to look hot to these people. I want to look like a mom," I protested, fingering it. It was long enough, as far as sundresses went, but I couldn't wear a bra with it because of a plunging neckline and spaghetti straps.

"Nothing wrong with being a hot mom."

I smiled at him and grabbed it. He held up one of my thongs with the other hand. I grabbed it and shimmied into it, then pulled the dress over my head. I looked into the mirror. "Are you sure?"

He slid onto the bed, leaning back, scrutinizing me, and shook his head slowly.

I gave him a doubtful look.

He reached for me, his fingers walking their way under the dress, caressing my ass. "Not sure I want to share you, looking that good."

I swatted him away, but only half-heartedly, now, because I loved the feeling of his hands on me. I wished I could enjoy it. I wished I didn't have to feel this goddamned need to make everything perfect. Why should I want to impress perfect people whose opinions of us and how we lived our lives shouldn't have mattered? "Cullen..."

He wrapped his hands around my bottom, squeezed, and stared up at me. Then he let go. "All right. I'm ready when you are."

I looked at him. Yes, he looked good, the way I liked him. Even in a clean white shirt, he still managed to look dirty. He was tatted and rough and beautiful... but what would the country club set next door think?

I knew Cullen could be charming, but if he got somewhere where he felt disrespected, he put up a fight. I didn't want him to turn into an asshole. I didn't even want to think about the possibility of him creating a scene next door, among the people I so desperately wanted to befriend.

But no, he was right. I had him, I had Ella, and those were the people who mattered. Everyone else could fuck off. I scuffed into my flip-flops, straightened my back, and took a deep breath. "I'm ready."

I went across the hall and woke Ella, who'd fallen asleep. I woke her and slipped a fresh new sundress on her and checked my phone. Only twenty minutes late. Not too bad.

"Can you get the potato salad from the fridge for me?" I asked as I hefted Ella's overflowing diaper bag onto my shoulder.

He went into the kitchen to grab it for me and I had to laugh a little when I saw him, all cool in his dark sunglasses and jeans . . . holding Tupperware under one arm.

We went outside and down the long driveway to the sidewalk. The road was already choked with cars, as was the Sumter's long, U-shaped driveway. Barry had a high fence up around the backyard, but I could hear the chatter of people, along with smooth jazz music, wafting up over the barrier.

I looked at Cullen, and he reached over and took my hand. I entwined my fingers with his as he said, "We'll be fine."

When he looked at me like that, with that commanding Cullen expression, it was impossible to believe anything bad could ever happen to us.

"Do you think we should go in the front, or around back?"

He shrugged, slipped off his sunglasses, and hung them in the neck of his t-shirt. I walked toward the front door, and started to reach for the doorbell, when he stepped in front of me and said, "Before you do that..."

I looked down at myself. I figured I had a hair out of place, or the tag of my dress was hanging out, and he was just going to tuck it where it belonged.

Instead, he set the Tupperware down.

CULLEN

He reached into his pocket.

And as he knelt on one knee, I thought for sure that he must have dropped something.

I just stared, mouth open. He wasn't proposing. This was Cullen. He was the Cobras President. And this was our neighbor's doorstep.

"I've been wanting to do this for a couple days, baby," he said, scratching the side of his face. "But you know me. Always late for just about everything. Doesn't mean I don't love you. Because I do. I love you and Ella more than anything. You two turned my world upside down in the best of ways and I'll be damned if I'll let you get away from me again."

Okay. Unless my ears were really playing tricks on me, that sounded a little like a proposal.

He held the ring out in his hand. It was a perfect, heart-shaped solitaire, exactly what I probably would've picked out myself . . . had I ever thought this day would come.

But I never had. This was Cullen McKnight, after all.

I just stared. Cullen McKnight. Proposing. To me. It didn't compute. All I kept thinking was. Party. At the Sumter's. I made potato salad. And . . . now he was kneeling in front of me, with a ring.

He took my hand and gazed up into my eyes. "Grace, will you marry me?"

That typical, intense, presidential gaze locked on mine. I didn't stand a chance. My knees wobbled. "You're proposing . . . to me?"

He shook his head.

Oh, okay. I thought for a second this was some weird, crazy miscommunication.

"To *both* of you. Ella, and you. I want you both to be my family."

Then the tears came. Hard. Showers and fountains and waterfalls of tears.

CULLEN

I shook my head. This wasn't happening. I mean, I'd made potato salad. I'd been all flustered. And now we were going to meet a bunch of total strangers and try to impress them and be good neighbors . . . and meanwhile, I had mascara all over my face and looked like a total wreck. "What is happening?" I blubbered. "Why . . ."

"Say yes, baby," he coaxed gently.

"Yes. Of course, yes! But I can't believe you're asking me this!" He slipped the ring onto my finger. "When did you decide? Why now?"

"I decided," he said, standing up and taking me and Ella into his arms. "When we left the Four Seasons. I got the ring a week ago. I'd tried to do it a dozen times but it was never the right time."

As he pulled me close, I stared at the ring. I was engaged. This was the fairy tale. The fairy tale I'd always wanted, but never in a million years thought would happen, with Cullen.

No. This was *better* than the fairy tale.

"Oh, my God. I can't believe it."

Just then, the door opened. Barry stood there, smiling at us. I waved my finger to tell her the impossible news when she looked at Cullen and said, "You get it done? Finally?"

He gave her a sheepish look and smiled. "I did it though, didn't I?"

What? They sounded entirely too familiar than I expected them to be. I stared at her, confused. She grinned at me. "He told me this morning he still hadn't done it, and I cracked my whip."

I closed my eyes, trying to make sense of what she was saying. "What . . . he told you? I thought . . ."

"You thought we hated each other?" Barry laughed. "Well, I suppose things were a little cool between us, up until a week ago, when he came over and told me his plans. Since then, we've been the best of friends."

"Friends?" My eyes volleyed back and forth between them. "His . . . plans?"

CULLEN

She nodded and opened the screen door. "Well, come on in! Everyone's waiting."

Cullen reached down to scoop up the potato salad and held the door open for me. I went through the house, in a daze, not sure what the hell was going on. I had a ring on my finger that told me I was going to marry Cullen. I was going to be his wife. My heart was jumping for joy and thrumming in my chest from sheer disbelief.

Barry led us to the kitchen, where she opened up the sliding glass doors and stepped aside, waving her hand with great flourish.

I moved into the doorway, having no clue what I'd see. A unicorn? After all, I'd already seen Cullen on a knee in front of me. After that, anything was possible.

The second I stepped out onto the deck, the cheer rose up from the crowd. "Congratulations!"

I looked around, stunned, at all the banners and balloons, all proclaiming the very same thing. Ella clapped her hands and pointed. "Balloon!"

My eyes scanned the crowd. There were the well-to-do, preppy types that I'd expected, and also, a number of men in jeans and *kuttes*, just like Cullen. Cobras. They were all mingling together, having a great time. They'd all known about this.

This was a party for us. An engagement party. And from the way Cullen was grinning at me, he'd known about it all along.

"You're a sneaky thing," I whispered to him between smiles. I'd never had a baby shower, a sweet sixteen, or anything even close to it. In fact, looking out at the sea of faces swarming around Barry's expansive yard, I realized it was the biggest party I'd ever been to, period.

And Cullen had done it, for me. For us.

I started to cry, all over again.

We walked down the steps and he greeted his men, introducing me to all of them, whose names I quickly forgot. Some of them hugged me, and the congratulations went up all around. It was easy to see

CULLEN

that these men not only respected Cullen—they loved him. They were the only family he knew.

Barry introduced us to her friends and family, who were just as nice as she'd been to me, and all the while, I couldn't get over that this was what it was like to finally fit in. This was our new normal. A little bit crazy, a little bit wild. Not your typical fairy tale, but a fairy tale nonetheless. I had a feeling Ella and I could definitely get used to it.

"Thank you," I whispered to Cullen, when we'd finally had a minute alone and he put a beer in my hand. I clinked my bottle with his and took a drink.

He reached into my diaper bag and pulled out a sippy cup, which he handed to Ella. "Anything for my girls," he said.

I smiled at him as Ella reached out her arms to him and crawled into his embrace. "Daddy," she said, tugging his beard.

EVIE MONROE

"That's right," I said, entwining my fingers with his. "He's your daddy. And I'm your mommy. And all of us, everyone here . . .we're your family."

THE END

Acknowledgements

Thank you to KB Winters for getting me into this mess. Thank you to all the ARC readers, Facebook fans and editors. Without all of you I wouldn't be able to do what I do.

Copyright © 2018 BookBoyfriends Publishing LLC

EVIE MONROE

About The Author

I love fairytales, princesses and bad boys. I just didn't realize how much until I started writing about them. I have found a new love in my life and I hope you have too!

You can find me here!

facebook.com/eviemonroeauthor/

eviemonroeauthor@gmail.com

eveimonroe.com

Copyright © 2018 BookBoyfriends Publishing LLC

Made in the USA
Middletown, DE
28 February 2019